THE DEATH
OF A
10-YEAR-OLD BOY

THE DEATH
OF A
10-YEAR-OLD BOY

A NOVEL

SCOTT REARDON

Aspen Press
25 Bleecker Street
New York, NY 10104

First Edition: December 2022
The publisher is not responsible for websites (or their content) that are not owned by the publisher.

ISBN: 979-8-9873738-0-4
LCCN: 2022921825
10 9 8 7 6 5 4 3 2 1
lsc-c
Printed in the United States of America

CHAPTER

THE BOY'S DOCTOR called, and the man answered. It was exactly as he and his wife feared. In fact, as the man later reflected, the test results were almost perfect in their annihilation. The growth had already spread. There was no point in operating. Chemo would only prolong the inevitable and at the cost of what little life the patient still had.

The man was too shocked to react. Then he was left with what a person is always left with: the practical.

"Well, what do people do in our situation?" he asked.

"They try to enjoy the time they have left."

The man had already told his wife. When he got home, they hugged and then discussed how to tell the boy. The man said he'd like to tell him, and his wife agreed.

The boy was at soccer practice, so the man waited in his room. The boy had a photo of him and his dad on a ship at

Mystic Seaport. The boy had once told him that was the best day of his life.

"Why?" the man had asked.

"Because that was when my bucket was the most full."

"How full was it?"

"Ninety-two percent."

"Whoa."

The boy had nodded gravely. "Yeah, that's about as full as it gets."

The man had been in the boy's bedroom thousands of times, but now he stared at his son's things, surprised that he'd missed all they had to reveal. There were posters on the wall of football players, warriors and almost unimaginable monsters. The boy wanted adventure and risk. He wanted to face something terrible beyond question, where a person's only choice was to fight back. Like all children, like all people, the boy desperately wished to be a hero. He knew already that was the most a human being could be.

And what did it mean exactly to be a hero?

It meant putting oneself at risk in the deepest, most personal way. The hero didn't do this for himself but for others or for principles which benefited others, but which perhaps only the hero believed. At his core, the hero stood for the idea that life meant something. He was always flawed, usually a bitter alcoholic or a cheerfully unconcerned womanizer. Yet he was a believer. And he stood for what every man, woman and child admired above all else. He stood for the glory of the human race. Of life itself. And it wasn't an earthly glory but cosmic glory against the universe, glory raised to the heavens to be seen by whatever higher power was out there.

What struck the man was how desperate and beautiful that was.

And yet it was absurd.

People watched TV, worked their jobs. But they wanted to be more than that. They wanted what no mortal thing could ever have: significance. And for the first time in his life, the man understood what a person really was. His son with all his hopes and dreams plastered on his wall was just like all people. He was brimming with decency and the desire for something great, yet he was ordinary and perishable. He was just a wish that was never coming true.

The boy came bounding in. He paused when he saw his dad, curious but pleasantly surprised.

"I have something really bad to tell you," the man said.

"Okay."

"Remember that thing the doctor found in your head?"

"Yes."

"It's cancer, and the doctor said it's going to kill you."
The boy said nothing.
"You have a month, maybe two."
"And then I'll die?"
"And then you'll die."
The boy remained very still. He just stood there, utterly alone. It was astonishing how all alone the boy suddenly was.
"Could there be a mistake?" the boy asked.
"It's unlikely. They double-checked everything."
"I feel fine though. I mean, I feel really good."
"People who have what you have usually do at this stage."
The man waited for the boy to say something else, but he just stood there frozen. Only when the man hugged him was the boy able to cry. And as they held each other, the man looked at the child in his arms. He was so real and one-of-a-kind, and he could be taken away so easily that the man almost couldn't stand it.

That night, after putting the boy and his younger sister to bed, the man and the wife laid together unable to sleep.
"Do we keep sending him to school?" the man's wife asked.
"He told me once if he had an army, he'd shell Robert Frost Elementary to the ground."
They both laughed.

5

"He also told me school made him hate things," the man said. "The teachers and the other kids were always coming down on someone. He said all school taught him was that life is just rules."

"God, he's not wrong."

"No. Maybe he should go a few more days. But then I don't think we should send him back there."

The man's wife nodded. "Okay."

CHAPTER

WHEN THE SCHOOL found out about the boy's diagnosis, the teachers insisted on holding a celebration of the boy's life. The man and his wife were moved beyond words. The school had planned a two-hour-long event. Apparently the parents of the other children also insisted on attending.

When the man and his wife arrived, the classroom was filled to the brim with children and adults. And the man almost couldn't help it. His heart swelled in a way that hurt, yet felt incredible. Another class came in and sang a song. Then the students took turns reading letters they'd written about his son. Some were sad and made everyone cry. Others were funny and made everyone laugh. The gist of them was that his son was a lot of fun, yet he always had to figure things out on his own and could be stubborn as hell.

Soon, though, the man began to grow uncomfortable.

The things said about his son were so generic they revealed

nothing of the boy's true depths. In fact they reminded the man of how a researcher on TV had once described the different personalities of lab rats. A girl got up and talked about how his son was funny and independent yet mischievous. And the man thought of how the researcher had described Subject #17 as the "class clown." Meanwhile Subject #34 was the "skeptic." These superficial descriptions only reinforced the truth about each rat's existence: that its character was entirely superfluous to its function.

Listening to the students and the teachers, the man began to feel that his son was just one body filling a seat among hundreds. This particular body had a mildly amusing personality. But soon another child would fill the seat. This new one would perhaps cause thirty percent less laughter but also thirty percent fewer disruptions.

Something else began to bother the man even more though.

There was a cheerful tone to what was said that wasn't meant for his son. It was meant for the people who in a month or two would still be alive. And he realized the true purpose of the class celebration. His son's death was meant to be used as inspiration to the living.

He could tell the other parents, in particular, had attended for this reason. The man and his wife lived in a wealthy town filled with people who worked long hours for money and position. Life had gone right for them. And what consumed people for whom life had gone right were things that made a statement about them, things that raised their place in the hierarchy: the right schools, the right house, the correct beliefs, knowing the best people. The man had always wondered why he'd never quite liked where he lived, and he realized it was a place where everything was meant to have an effect on other people.

He and his wife had always been on the outskirts of the town's competitive social scene. Now the other parents spoke to them as though they'd secretly been friends all along. They offered heartfelt outpourings of sympathy. But they'd always watch the man and his wife closely. And the man realized the other parents were there out of curiosity. They wanted to get close to death, not out of concern for the dying but to motivate themselves to extract everything they could out of their own lives.

Now that he'd seen it, he couldn't unsee it. The man's wife gave him a look. She'd begun to see it too. They stayed another hour, trying not to feel fed upon and doing their best to smile and look on the bright side.

On the ride home, the man's wife attempted to be positive. "That was really nice, wasn't it?"

The boy said nothing. Before, they would have scolded him

9

for not being positive enough.

"Yes," the boy said finally. "That was nice."

CHAPTER

THE MAN sat on the train, and the boy sat next to him. The boy had an appointment with a doctor in the city. When the train doors opened, they merged into the crowd and made their way to the hospital.

The waiting room was on the top floor, towering so high over the city that nothing below looked real. It was one of those modern designs where all the specialties were served by a single waiting room. The result was a child with an ear infection could be sitting next to one dying of bladder cancer.

The boy was assigned to Section 4.

They sat watching the other patients come and go.

A nurse called his son's name, and they were led through a labyrinth of hallways to an exam room. The doctor came in through yet another door. He walked them through what to expect, wrote several prescriptions and asked if they had any questions. Everything was so final the man didn't know what he could possibly ask.

Strangely he turned to his son. "Do you have any questions?"

Do you have any questions about the fact you're going to die in a month?

The boy seemed to sense that there weren't any true answers to his questions and that, as a result, it would be rude to waste everyone's time. He shook his head no. What surprised the man was that he was grateful for this.

The man took the boy back to the train station and watched him depart. He'd tried to talk to the boy, but another person was always too close. It never seemed to be the right moment. And for some reason, the man felt embarrassed the way he had in the doctor's office. The boy seemed to feel it too. And what struck the man was how monstrous that was: to have to die quietly. Politely.

As the man left the station, he looked at all the people around him, all the giant institutions, all the forward motion, and he hated the silence they enforced. He hated how they'd made him silent too. And, most of all, he hated that at the moment of truth, it was the silence he'd listened to and not his son.

That afternoon, the man sat in his office, unable to work, staring out at the enormity of midtown.

The boy had been sent back to school, and instead of going

home, the man had decided to come in. He thought about that a long time. It was interesting how reluctant the family was to abandon the sources of its normalcy. The boy's life without school, sports, without preparation for a lifetime of advancement, was impossible to imagine. And the man wondered, *Was this it? Were achievement and status the sum of my son's life?*

He opened his door and looked out over the office. Everything that had once animated his life now seemed so unimportant and remote. Even though he was really just functionary, the man had always liked his job. He was a value investor, and he placed massive bets on things when no one else was interested in them. It was a card game you played against the world. That was what he loved. The world was always trying to kill you. And your job wasn't just to survive, it was to strike back. To prevail.

It was the biggest game there was: a polite, socially-blessed form of warfare that sucked in more players than any other. And the stakes were enormous. People who labored for a living, whether they were construction workers or cardiologists, labored their entire lives. Only those who could make money from money itself could win their freedom. So that's what the players were competing for: self-ownership. If you won, you thought large thoughts, and your time was your own. And if you lost, you rode the train to work and spent the rest of your days serving others in exchange for the things on which your survival depended. Many of the players loved the money, but the man only wanted the freedom—for himself, for his children.

But was this it?

He'd groomed the boy for the exact same life as his. They spoke often of virtue, but really this was just a means of getting ahead. They'd told the boy about being brave and being good. But bravery, when it stopped being an abstraction, meant risking embarrassment and was almost never the smart move. Meanwhile being good usually meant nothing more than fitting in or putting another person's demands above your own. And what struck the man was how little he'd truly given his son.

He wondered what the boy was doing at that exact moment.

His son was so calm on the outside, yet inside he was doing the lonely, nameless work of dying. Every waking moment, he was probably trying to understand what was happening to him, trying to figure if maybe it could be something other than what it was. And he was looking to others for answers they simply didn't have.

The man pictured his son's wide, searching eyes. They held the look that every child's eyes hold. The look that said, *Do I really matter?*

Does someone love me?

Does something out there care about me at all?

The man's office phone rang. He stared at it, mystified.

When it rang again, he walked out of the building.

On the train home, the man thought about the time left. And he thought about what his son desperately wished for. More than anything, his son wished to live. Not exist. Not survive another day. He wished to live. And the man wondered, *Can you give someone a life in just thirty days?*

CHAPTER

WHEN THE MAN got home, he found the boy crying in his room.

"What's wrong?" he asked.

"Caleb, Ben and Hunter are going on a fishing trip in a few months. When I asked them about it, they all got quiet. Finally they said there really wasn't any point in telling me about it because I wouldn't be around. Then some other kids started laughing."

It was almost scary how well the man could picture this. And it was amazing how easily tragedy could turn a person into an outcast.

"Do I have to keep going to school?" the boy asked.

Before the man could speak, the boy said, "Please don't make me go back there. It's like…"

"It's like what?"

"It's like everyone's waiting to see what's going to happen

to me."

The boy lost the composure he'd been maintaining for days and reached for his dad with both arms.

The man hugged him back. "You don't have to go back there ever again, okay?"

"Okay."

They kept hugging.

"Dad?"

"Yeah."

"Thank you."

"Yeah."

"Will you lay with me tonight?"

"Of course."

The next morning, the man asked the boy what he'd always wanted to do.

"There's so much. I want to hunt a giant snake in the Congo. I want to go to Alaska. Put out a forest fire. Shoot a machine gun. Crash a semi."

"You want to crash a semi?"

The boy's eyes lit up. "Yeah, right into the music room at my school."

They all laughed.

The boy continued listing things. The man and his wife

looked at each other as the boy went on and on. They became still as if either moved, both would shatter.

The man went over to the boy and leaned down. "Listen, I want you to do something."

"What?"

"I want you to take a day and think the hardest you ever have in your life. Then I want you to tell us: if you could only do one thing before you die, what would that be? And when you think about the life you would have had, what would you have wanted to get out of it?"

The next morning, the boy came downstairs.

"Let's go to Montana," he said.

"Montana?"

"Remember that movie we saw about a boy and his dad in the frontier days? The rest of the family got killed by Indians, and they had to survive out in the wilderness all on their own. For years after that, we used to talk about taking a hunting trip in Montana, just you and me."

"Okay."

The boy raised his hands in innocence. "Here's the thing though. I read an article about a bear that's killed three people. Its range is huge, so they're organizing a hunting party to hunt it down. What if we helped and made it so it couldn't hurt anyone anymore?"

"I don't know," the boy's mother said.

The boy watched them. When he spoke, his voice wavered with feeling. "Part of the hunt takes place in open country. They say it's country that in places no one's ever been to before. I've always wanted to do that. Go where no one else has ever been."

"Why?" the man asked.

"To go as far as a person can." The boy thought a moment. "I've always wanted to go to the edge of the world—and then just keep going."

The man watched the boy, saddened that such incredible things existed deep inside his son and only now was he getting to see them.

"What about the other thing?" the man asked.

"What other thing?"

"When you think about the life you would have had, what would you have wanted to get out of it?"

The boy became quiet again. Then he said, "I don't know, Dad. I just know I want something. Does that make sense?"

The man spoke in a whisper. "Yeah."

The man and his wife laid in bed together.

"What if something happens to him?" the man's wife asked.

"You mean what if the grizzly eats him two weeks before

the cancer does?"

The man's wife laughed once. She couldn't help it. Now that their worst fears had come true, a gallows humor had taken hold in them both.

"It sounds dangerous," the man's wife said.

"It isn't a real adventure without real risk."

The man's wife considered this.

The man touched her hand. "The truth is if something happens, then I will have robbed you and him of several weeks of his life."

"That isn't very much."

"I'm hoping it's a lot."

Neither spoke for a moment.

"Are you sure you don't want to come?" the man asked.

"I can't come."

The man said nothing.

"There's something he needs from you before he dies."

"What?"

"I don't know. I don't think he knows. But I see the way he looks at you, even when someone else is talking. He needs something, and you're the only one who can give it to him."

"You know what I like about you?" the man said. "You seem so normal. But underneath there's this wild thing."

The woman laughed. For a moment, she looked like the girl

she'd once been before children and middle age. The one whose troubles hadn't found her yet. She looked beautiful to him then—as he realized so much in her had already died as well.

CHAPTER

THE MAN AND THE BOY landed in Missoula and headed to the campsite. The man looked out the car window. Being in Montana was like stepping into the ancient past, all of it. In Montana's blank wide-open spaces, he could feel in his chest the planet's endless oceans of time.

The landscape even dwarfed the buildings, as if it was slowly swallowing everything people had built. This was a place that existed beyond things like laws and civilization, beyond the human race's religious belief in itself.

At the lodge, they went in to register.

The lobby was cavernous and opulent in an Old West way. The man looked around. There was no one here. And there was something eerie, almost post-apocalyptic, about a place that ought to have been bustling yet was completely empty. Their footsteps echoed as they walked, and the man didn't like disturbing all that emptiness.

Someone was standing behind the front desk. The man hadn't seen anyone, yet the old man stood as though he'd been there the whole time.

"May I help you?" the old man asked.

"Where is everyone?"

"Up at camp."

"We wanted to sign in."

The old man produced some paperwork, and the man filled it out and then signed his name.

"This is the third one," the old man said. "Hopefully you all have more luck than the people that came before."

"The third one?"

"Well, actually it's more like the fourth. Some people tried to hunt the Old One a decade ago. They didn't get anywhere either."

"The Old One? The newspapers said the bear was a young rogue male."

"Could be. Some of us old-timers, though, think it was the Old One."

"Why's that?"

The old-timer eyed the man's son. "Not sure I should say in front of the boy."

"He can handle it."

"Ten years ago, some spiritual types set up a town past the

Voreland Gate. Folks told them not to, but they were determined. They built a town hall, a church unlike anything you've ever seen. But that October, a flash blizzard hit. Snowed them into the valley. They call that area Skinner's Crossing. It's a hunting ground for grizzlies and wolves, also a proving ground once for the Sioux. They were trapped with nine adult grizzlies. Those people didn't believe in guns, and it was almost time for the bears to hibernate." The old man's words caught a little in his throat. "The animals—well, they were ravenous."

The man looked at his son. The boy was motionless as he stared at the old man.

"After the spring thaw, no one came down," the old man continued. "Some folks went up and discovered them. They shot all the bears except for the Old One, who escaped."

"Is the town still there?" the boy asked.

"I reckon so. But no one's been up there."

"Why not?"

"It's remote. Sixty miles on foot. Also you know how people are."

As they left, the old man pulled the man aside. "Listen, they discovered gold on the Indian reservation up there. Some of you are going to be near the mine. My recommendation, mister: don't go near the reservation. Don't go near the gold mine."

"Why not?"

But the old man just stood there with an odd look on his face, one that bothered the man long after they'd left because there was something terrible in it.

The man and the boy boarded the shuttle, which took them through a dark forest and then up into the hills. The staging ground was an old logging camp with cabin dormitories and a large mess hall. Men and boys huddled inside the main tent. It was like hunting camp from the 1920s. Once again, the man had an overwhelming feeling of having gone back in time.

They were told the director running the hunt wouldn't arrive for a few more hours.

A group of men huddled in the mess hall, exchanging stories and gossip.

One of the men had scarred hands from clawing a livelihood out of the earth. His eyes and skin were yellowish like he was sick, yet his movements were quick and lively as though he could overpower biological realities through inhuman force of will.

The man turned to the boy. "This your first hunt?"

"Yes, sir."

"Where you from?"

"Connecticut."

"This will be very different from Connecticut."

The boy said nothing.

"They say it's federal land. But that land out there is older than governments. Older than the idea of property itself."

"Are you a hunter?" the boy asked.

"Since I was your age." The man turned and said to the others, "This is this young man's first hunt. He could have taken potshots at deer from a yacht in Connecticut. Instead he came here to the end of the earth with us."

The others said nothing, but strange looks came across their faces, as though the hunter had invoked something important.

"Hunting here is where a young person joins the great game," the hunter said.

"The great game?"

"The only way to survive is to kill other things. Up until now, your killing has been done for you." The man was quiet a moment. "I'll bet you don't know why you came here, why it called to you. But we can tell you. You came to do your own killing. You came to find out what you are. And to do that, you have to spin the wheel and play. Out here, you can't kill without maybe getting killed yourself. That's the great game, the game of chance and skill man has always played against the universe and always will."

"I'm not scared," the boy said.

"You will be. And that's a good thing. Only bottomless

terror can keep you sharp enough to survive."

The hunter fell silent and joined the others in staring at the boy.

For a moment, the man both pitied and envied his son. He pitied him because he was dying, yet life made no exceptions. He still had to walk through the fire. But the man envied him because the boy was being initiated into something that had been here long before him and would still be here long after. And as the men's reticence showed, this was something sacred, something beyond the reach of such a weak and dishonest thing as words.

A caravan of old pickups roared into camp. Everyone began to congregate in the main tent.

The director took the stage. "Thank you all for coming. This is the third one of these we've done, and so far we've had no luck. Hopefully we can turn it around. First of all, everything you've heard about the bear is true. Everyone it's attacked, it's killed. Two people have died this year alone. And we know the attacks weren't defensive because their remains were partially consumed. Once a bear discovers a source of food, it never forgets. And this bear's smart. He has an usually large range, and he moves within it like a ghost.

"Some think this was one of the bears involved in the attack on the Crossing. But there's no real evidence of that other than the bear's age. Bears typically live twenty years. This one appears to be almost thirty, which is incredible because it's one of the largest on record.

"We'll hand out pictures, but the bear's main identifying feature is the shock of white fur across its back. Now the rest of you are drawing lots to get assigned a patrol area. But someone needs to go all the way up north, through the Voreland Gate, right up to the Crossing. The whole thing's inaccessible by vehicle, so you'll have to hoof it. Any volunteers?"

No one raised their hand. Then all the eyes turned. The boy had raised his.

The director looked at the man. "That work for you, Dad?"

The man nodded.

"It isn't safe up there without a guide," the director said. "We know a good one if you're agreeable to it."

"We'd appreciate that."

The director looked at the crowd. "We just got an update from the weather service. Some weather's appeared. The storm's predicted to hit in three days. If it stays on course, everyone needs to evac. You don't want to be out there in this." He eyed the crowd as if waiting for someone to challenge him. Then his face softened. "One last thing. Everyone, stay safe out there. It isn't just this bear that's dangerous. They all are. Now god bless, you sons-of-bitches." He waved his hat, and there was some scattered applause.

Everyone began to mount up. Men checked their munitions and their other supplies. Others started up gigantic ATVs, lashed rations to the back and then roared off.

The director approached the man. "You get in trouble or you need to evac, there's one road up there. You'll have to walk a fair way, but there's a town, and they got a diner and a shitty little three-room motel."

"How come no one else raised their hand?" the man asked.

"There used to be a settlement up there. It's a ghost town now, and the thought of it makes folks a little uneasy."

"That the one the bears attacked?"

"Ah, you heard about it already."

"A little."

"Well, it's also far. Nothing up there for hundreds of miles. Listen, you seem like a nice fella. You sure you want to go all the way up to a place like that? And with a kid? We could just hire somebody."

"I'm sure."

The director just looked at him, not saying anything for a moment. Then he said, "I don't know your experience, but you should know something. When people go that deep into the wild, it does something to them."

"Like what?"

"They see things. They get so alone it changes them."

"You been out there?"

"Yes, sir."

"It really that bad?"

"It was the most incredible thing I've ever seen, but it took something. That's all I can say." His eyes hardened. "You can go too far. And it killed something in me."

For a moment, both men were silent.

Then the director said, "That guide I mentioned is already here. One of my men will take you to him. But listen, my advice. That ghost town up there, don't go near it. And don't stay up there any longer than you have to."

Their guide was a gigantic Sioux man named Bragg.

He handed the man a device. "That's your emergency beacon in case we get separated."

"Anything else?"

"Let's get a move on to stay ahead of this storm."

They cut through the dark forest. In places, light couldn't penetrate the canopy, and everything was coated in mud. It was like walking through the bottom of a lake that had just been drained. There weren't even any animal sounds, and the man had the feeling that he was leaving one world and entering another.

When they came out of the forest, they stood on an overlook. Mountains and valleys stretched as far as the eye could see. The landscape was so large it was as though if they entered it, they might just disappear.

Bragg led them down. Once they'd reached level ground, they began to cross a giant plain. The man caught himself looking for a telephone pole. A road. But he couldn't imagine anything as normal as a road ever existing here.

"It's like an inoculation," Bragg said. "It either takes hold in you right away, or it never does."

They both watched the boy, who'd been moved to silence.

"He can't believe it," the man said. "It's like something out of a movie."

"It's bigger than any movie," Bragg replied. "Bigger than any person's imagination."

"I had no idea there was any place left that was like this."

"This really is the last frontier. All the others are just water at the bottom of the ocean or miles and miles of sand. We've left the roads. Soon we'll even leave the trails. We're going to places no one's been in hundreds of years. In some of the places, maybe no one's been there ever."

They'd only been out a few hours. But already the wild had them. And everything else, the man's job, his wife, even his daughter back at home, all of it was gone. Just gone.

The man pulled up alongside the boy. "Is it what you hoped?"

"It's more than I hoped." The boy's voice was soft.

"Do you still want to kill the bear?"

"I feel like we have to."

"Why's that?"

"Back at camp, the man said once a bear discovers a food source, it never abandons it. Eventually that bear's going to kill again."

"But what do *you* want? That's what I'd like to know. Do you want to hunt it?"

The boy thought a moment and nodded. "It's like, I don't know the word. It's like the bear and us were always supposed to meet."

"Destiny."

"Yes. Destiny."

"There's a very good chance we won't find it, you know that?"

"I know."

"Then we will have wasted the little time we still have."

"We won't have wasted it. Not to me."

The man watched his son. The boy had always had a quiet, unself-conscious goodness. It was amazing how different the man experienced his two children. His daughter was this incredible little stranger. But when he looked at his son, he felt like he was looking at a version of himself. And when he witnessed the boy's triumphs and struggles, he felt he was looking at a repetition of his own life. On one hand, it was a gift to see your past lived by someone else. On the other, it was haunting—because there was so little you could change.

As they walked, Bragg and the man studied the map. Bragg traced their route. His finger circled around a small area called Smuggler's Cragg.

"Why are we going around that?" the man asked.

"Not a good area."

"What is it?"

Bragg hesitated.

"That's the gold mine, isn't it?" the man said.

"You don't want to see the mine."

"Why is everyone so funny about that place?"

"They can't get equipment to the pit. The terrain's one giant impasse."

"Then how are they digging?"

"They've got some equipment, but mostly they're doing it by hand."

Coldness ran through the man's heart. "That's medieval. It'd take thousands of workers."

"And that's what the mining corporation has. It's owned by the res. The government gave them a grant, and they used it to import a labor force. Mostly illegals, other Indians and white men who've fallen on hard times."

Silence as both men caught their breath to keep up the pace.

"It's said to be a place where men lose their souls. Before, there was nothing waiting for you if you fell far enough in the world. Now, they say, there's the mine."

"We'd still like to see it," the man said.

"What about your boy?"

"I think he should see it too."

Bragg looked up in surprise. The two men stared at each other.

"If you want to go to the mine, we have to go through the mining camp," Bragg said. "It's the only way. You sure you want that?"

"I'm sure."

Bragg watched the man, not understanding. Then he stared at the boy, and after a moment, it was as though he'd found his answer.

Bragg sped up and walked ahead until they made camp that night.

After the boy had gone to bed, the man sat with Bragg in the glow of the fire.

"Your son's sick, isn't he?" Bragg said.

"Yes."

The man was quiet for a moment. "Have you been to that town where those people died?"

"No one's been back up there. Why?"

But the man shook his head.

Bragg stared off. "My ancestors felt the Crossing was a very spiritually active place. They believed everything has a spirit, and that spirit must be expressed. They'd go there to dance with the spirits."

"The spirits of what?"

"Of the trees. Of their own ancestors. Of the place itself."

"That what you think too?"

Bragg grinned. "I believe what modern people believe. I don't believe in anything at all."

"But the tourists love to hear that stuff."

"They sure do."

The man smiled sadly. "I'm just like them, I suppose. I want it to be true."

"I have some family who still believe. The poorest ones. The worst off. People come from the wealthiest, most advanced places in the world to see them and their ways. These wealthy people worked tooth and nail to pull their societies out of the conditions in which my family still lives. And now that they've reached the peak, they're so disenchanted they want to go all the way back to the bottom. Think about that."

"What do you think about it?"

"This is a world without answers. A world desperate for them."

Both men stared up at the stars in the sky.

The man spotted Orion's Belt. "They say we're only twenty years away from leaving our solar system."

"You think they'll find anything out there?"

"No, and that's probably the greatest horror of all."

"What's so bad about that?"

The man stared off. "That we're it. That once a meteor or something else hits the planet, all memory will be gone. And the whole thing just resets. The dinosaurs were here for 180 million years. People have only existed for 100,000. Maybe we aren't God's children. Maybe we're just another blip on the radar."

The man was silent again.

"I've been thinking about my son, about everything. And I've realized it isn't all leading somewhere."

"What do you mean?"

"Like with the tourists who visit your family. We sacrifice and break ourselves because we think someday it'll be better.

And even if we don't have the answers, we'll at least be farther along. But there's no progress. There isn't even any escape. It's all just a giant loop feeding back on itself."

"Escape from what?"

"Pardon?"

"What is it you think we all want to escape from?"

"The truth." A haunted look came across the man's face. "About what we really are. What all of this really is."

Bragg stared at him. "I feel sorry for the boy. But I feel even sorrier for you."

"For me?"

"You're in a situation most people never find themselves in."

The man said nothing.

"Because you're out here, and you're all alone. Because you've seen past all the pretty lies, and you no longer believe in a single thing."

CHAPTER

THEY REACHED the Cragg at noon.

Bragg stood waiting for them at a fork in the path.

He pointed to a forest below them. "To reach the mine, we need to head down there."

"We're ready," the man said.

They proceeded down. When the land leveled off, the forest ended suddenly. All the trees had been either chopped down or dynamited. Their wasted remains littered the ground. It was like the site of a mass murder.

The mining camp was a tent city. Rows of them dotted the outskirts with some configured into tiny neighborhoods. Large white tents formed a downtown along Main Street. Footsteps had reduced the street to mud and puddles of waste water, which the residents trudged through without concern.

In a makeshift bar, several tables of men sat drinking and playing cards. An enclosure of port-a-potties had been constructed outside. A man emerged from one and vomited into the street before returning to the bar and ordering another drink.

As the man and the boy came into view, the men in bar stopped and stared, their eyes like holes which nothing, not even the entire world, would ever fill.

A man watched the boy and said something in a language so foreign-sounding it could have come from another planet. The other men began to laugh.

"What did he say?" the man asked Bragg.

"It's not important."

"What did he say?"

"He said that in his current state, the boy is the most beautiful woman he's ever seen."

The man turned to look back, but Bragg grabbed his arm. "Don't react. You can't win, only lose here."

At the edge of town, men stood in lines outside three tents. Every few moments, a man would emerge from a tent, zipping up his pants. Then another man would go inside. During one interchange, the man saw a woman inside the tent.

He and the woman locked eyes. And for a moment, they were two people on opposite sides of circumstance. The woman stared at him with the same look as the men.

The man reached over and touched his son, confirming

him in some way.

They paused outside of town. Only once their bodies suddenly relaxed did they realize how tense they'd been the entire time.

"The mine's just over the hill," Bragg said.

They crested the top, and when they looked down, the man's breath caught in his throat. What he saw was so alien it could only be understood in installments. The strip mine was a crater that had been sunk a quarter mile into the ground. It was like a pit in the middle of the Amazon. Things were crawling all over it the way bees swarm a hive. And it took the man a moment to realize that these were people.

Hundreds of them.

The weather was warm, and the men laboring below had their shirts off. Each was covered head to toe in mud. The only part of them that seemed human were their teeth and the whites of their eyes. Gigantic ladders had been bolted to the walls of the crater, each the size of a football field. At any one time, at least a hundred men were scaling the ladders with sacks of dirt lashed to their backsides. The sacks were so heavy that when the men reached the top, some could no longer bear the weight and collapsed gradually with each step to the ground.

Something deep inside the man wanted to make it stop. And it all came to him in an instant. What he saw was the entire history of the human race. He saw the slave labor camps of the Nazis and the communists. He saw the seas of peasants chained and lashed by great empires—the Romans, the Greeks and all the others that people still spoke of with admiration. He saw the palace eunuchs in the Middle East, free people reengineered into model servants by their own biology. He saw the human chattel shipped to the new world, worked for a lifetime, then forced to breed their replacements. And he remembered there was no high-watermark of culture, no height of civilization, that didn't stand on the back of a mass labor force.

And he thought, *My god, this is it. This is all of us.*

This was a species consuming and defiling a world that was itself consuming and defiling them. This was a world of conquest and victory, gilded with imaginary concepts like mercy and justice which the victors used to cloak themselves with morality, the better to cement their gains.

To cross the mine, they had to circumvent its pitface. Hundreds of men blocked their path, their faces dirty and humanoid. As they weaved around them, not daring to meet the men's eyes, the men turned and stared. A fight broke out. A homeless-seeming man screamed at another man. Then some sort of overseer walked over and, without expression, clubbed the screaming man across the face. Afterward the screaming man reflected a moment and then resumed his work.

Once they were past the mine, a cheer went up among the miners, who were happy the interlopers had left.

The man looked back one last time. And he thought, *We're little and weak and could be crushed at any moment. You'd think it'd make us merciful. But we're truly the ugliest thing to ever exist. We're the monsters we've always feared. And if we were gods, we'd unleash the greatest hell the world has ever seen.*

As they walked away, the man was shaky because he knew what he'd just witnessed: the horror of the world his son would soon be leaving.

"It's worse than you ever thought," Bragg said.

"That's not it."

"Then what are you thinking?"

"It's true. That's why it's so bad." The man looked over. "It's true."

CHAPTER

THEY WERE HALFWAY to the Voreland Gate when the storm alerts began. Bragg's satellite phone kept beeping, each urgent new warning seeming to interrupt the last.

"Storm's thirty-six hours away," Bragg said. "We can keep going, but we're going to have to bed down up at Hanover."

"What's Hanover?"

"The last outpost. There's nothing after that."

"Is there a place to stay?"

"Only one motel. We have to hope they still have rooms."

"Will they?"

Bragg thought a moment. "Most people are evacuating. No one else is up here. They'll have room."

The man looked at the boy. "Do you want to risk it?"

"Yes." That was all the boy said.

They kept going.

They crested another hill. At the top, they stood overlooking a valley. The largeness of it, its giganticness, made the man feel like they'd fallen to their knees before something great. Except it wasn't a bad thing to fall on your knees. It was a relief—because they'd always wished for such a thing to exist.

The man wondered what the coming storm would be like. He'd only experienced storms in New England. This one would be different. New England was so forested you could only see a few hundred yards of the storm. But here they'd be able to see the whole thing. It'd be like the earth was going to war with itself, and they'd be caught in the middle.

Which was exactly what he wanted.

As they hiked down, Bragg stopped and pointed at tracks. "This is a moose run. We have to be careful. They're almost as dangerous as the bears."

The run had been cleared of foliage. The rest of the terrain was almost impassable, so they took the path even though it was dangerous. And the man could see how animals often lost their lives for the smallest convenience.

As the sun set, the light became soft, and the forest went quiet. It was like everything had paused from being itself. And there was a moment of reflection between the day and all its labors and the night and all its mysteries.

Bragg froze. "Get down."

The man and the boy crouched. Bragg remained motionless, staring at something. The path was only five yards wide. Bragg pointed to the tree-line a few feet away, and they all hid behind the trees.

Bragg spoke in a whisper. "No matter what, don't move. This is one of the biggest I've ever seen."

They watched the path. For a while, nothing happened, and the man almost couldn't stand the anticipation.

Then it appeared.

The first thing he saw were the antlers. They must have been eight feet apart. And they were so high off the ground the man couldn't believe they belonged to something that hadn't gone extinct long ago. When the moose came into view, it was so large and powerful that its body gave off an energy which made the man's hairs stand on end.

Its shoulders were taller than any person he'd ever seen. And its head reached just below the height of a basketball hoop. The man felt the most intoxicating fear he'd ever felt in his life. The boy just stared at the animal and was so still he didn't seem to be breathing. The animal walked past. Both the boy and the man gripped the trees, which were the only thing protecting them.

Only once the giant creature was out of sight could anyone in the hunting party become himself again.

Bragg looked at the boy. "Were you scared?"

The boy laughed. "Yes."

"Did you like it?"

The boy was quiet for a moment. Then he said, "That was one of the most incredible things that's ever happened to me."

Neither man spoke. They just stood watching the boy, reduced to silence the way adults only could be when a child reminded them how special and fragile it all was.

They made camp for the night. The man stayed up late thinking. Bragg had said he didn't believe in a single thing. The man sat turning that over in his mind. And he knew it was true.

He thought of the beliefs upon which his life had stood, the beliefs on which everyone's lives stood. Most people worshipped greatness—of their countries, their ideas, of their ancestors. But no nation, no people, no man-made creation had ever lasted. And three generations was all it took for your descendants to stop caring who or what you'd been. The believers in greatness sought immortality in something just as perishable as they were.

What struck the man was that everyone was clutching at the same thing. Everyone wanted to be the most real, the one who life was really all about. That was what they were actually screaming for when they screamed at the top of their lungs for freedom or equality or this god or that. They were screaming for themselves. And that was why they offed each other by the millions in the name of ideology. Each movement was convinced that if it could just achieve final victory over whatever stood in its way, they'd transcend life's broken reality. And they'd finally become what they worshipped. They'd finally be truth and justice and the highest, most immortal good there was.

And Bragg had been right. What the man saw was a giant dead end. He saw a planet of animals killing and dominating each other with their myths. Life wasn't the pursuit of happiness. It was the pursuit of realness. Every living thing was just a fiction bludgeoning and infecting and doing absolutely anything to become true.

The next morning, Bragg stood staring at something.

"What is it?" the boy asked.

"Wild apple trees," he said. "They feed dozens of animals, but the whole grove is about to be destroyed."

"By what?"

Bragg pointed at a gopher hole. "There's only one right now, but soon there'll be more." He turned to the boy. "Would you like to help me?"

"Sure."

Bragg walked over and placed a little cracker at the entrance of the hole. "When the gopher comes out, shoot it."

"But it isn't trying to kill the trees."

"No, but it'll still do a bad thing."

The boy waited by the hole for ten minutes. Then the man heard a gunshot. He came over, and the boy was watching the gopher writhe on the ground.

Its body finally went slack.

"That's the first thing I've ever killed," the boy said to no one.

Bragg and the man finished packing. As they left camp, the boy was still staring at the gopher.

Bragg patted the boy on the back. "You did the right thing."

"It looks so innocent."

"Innocent things die all the time. Usually that's why they die."

They'd only walked a few hours when Bragg stopped to read a message on his sat phone.

"Listen," he said. "We're not going to make it up to Hanover."

"Why not?"

"The storm's a category five. You see those ridges?" He pointed to the mountain ranges to the right and left of them. "Those turn this valley into a giant funnel. National Weather Service thinks there'll be a tornado. And if they think there's a tornado, there's going to be a tornado."

"It's two days back. If we leave, it'd take us five days just to get back here."

Bragg didn't seem to follow.

"We'd lose too much time," the man said.

"You could lose your lives."

"We're not leaving with you. We need to keep going."

"Why?"

The man looked off in the direction of the storm. "How bad will it be?"

"Listen, I have a family. Otherwise I'd consider—"

"We aren't asking you to stay. We'd never ask that."

Bragg leaned in. "Please. You could kill your son."

"I know that."

Bragg just stared at him. Then he pointed out into the distance. "The safest place is at the foot of the mountain. Too far up, you'll get blown off. Too far down, and you're in the storm's path. And avoid the rivers. Actually avoid any water. It'll rise. It's probably already rising. And it'll come for you. It'll take your life in slow motion."

The man nodded.

Bragg pointed to the horizon once more. "You can navigate using your beacon. But you can also navigate using the mountains. The ranges on each side of us run north-south. The

Voreland Gate is right between them, directly ahead. And if you get in trouble, Hanover is over those hills to the west, right at the foot of that miserable-looking peak."

Bragg asked to see the man's beacon. "If you get in trouble, use this. But you got to understand. No one's coming, not once it starts."

"We wouldn't want anyone putting themselves at risk because we've decided to lose our minds."

Bragg grinned. "That's what everyone says—before the storm."

The man grinned back.

"Okay," Bragg said. "Good luck."

"Thanks again."

The boy put out his hand, which Bragg shook.

"I'd love to take you both out another time," Bragg said. But then he caught himself and stopped speaking. He looked the boy in the eye and simply said, "It meant something to me, being out here with you."

"Me too," the boy said.

"Someone once told me that to say goodbye is to die a little." Bragg smiled. "Goodbye, young man."

"Goodbye, Mr. Bragg."

Bragg started to leave, then turned back toward the man. "You asked me about the town where those people died. I don't recommend going there. You have to go the whole way through the Cauldron. That's the most dangerous part of the hunting ground. I don't have the right to tell you what to do. But my recommendation: don't go all the way up to the Crossing. An entire town of people died in that place. God only knows what's up there."

Bragg waited for an assurance from the man, but the man said nothing.

Bragg turned, and they both watched him walk away until he'd disappeared.

The man squatted down next to his son. "Okay, this is it. In a few hours, it'll be too late to turn back."

The boy nodded like he understood and had always somehow understood. Then they turned, and they walked into the greatest unknown they'd ever imagined.

CHAPTER

STORM CLOUDS rolled in, giant thunderheads moving like something sent from a wrathful god.

The man and the boy were approaching the Kahnewald River, which they had to cross before the storm surge. The temperature had dropped, and the air became thick with the omen of rain. It was as though the atmosphere was about to burst into water.

"How long do we have?" the boy asked.

"Three hours."

"How far do we need to go?"

"Far."

They both stopped when they reached the river. Its waters had already swelled, and even from shore, the man could feel the power of the current. Everything Bragg had warned them about was already coming true. For a moment, the man's thoughts raced. They were stuck in the middle of the valley, the very place Bragg said they shouldn't be. But it was too late to turn back.

The boy had to shout over the crashing water. "Dad, what do we do?"

"Let me think."

The man looked up the river. It twisted and turned, the water colliding with the rocks so forcefully it sprayed up like a geyser. He looked the other way. The water was smoother downriver, which meant it was deeper. He stood trying to decide which risk to take: drowning down below or getting smashed on the rocks up above.

"We need to take off our clothes," he said.

"What?"

The man started to strip. "Take off your clothes."

"Why?"

"We're going down and swimming across."

Terror rose in the boy's eyes, but he started to undress. Like the man, he was scared of the river but even more scared of what was coming for them.

"Let me try it first," the man said. "If something happens, push this button on the beacon and start walking back."

"Dad, please don't leave me here. I'd rather be dead than have you leave me here."

The man watched the boy's face and suddenly understood.

"All right, here's what we'll do. I'll float in the water and see how strong it is. Then we'll go together. Okay?"

The boy was ready to take any deal. "Okay."

Naked, the man slid into the river. When he pushed away from the bank, he began to surge downstream but was able to swim back to shore.

"Give me your stuff," he said, climbing out of the water.

The boy handed him his backpack. The river narrowed here, and the man walked to its narrowest point. With all his might, he hurled the pack across the river where it landed barely on the other side. The man grabbed his pack and knew he couldn't throw it as far. He had to think.

Some logs formed a natural barricade in the water. The man took his pack and hurled it into the water, and the current trapped his pack against the logs.

He grabbed the boy's hand. "Let's go."

As they slipped into the river, the boy clung to his chest. And for a second, the man was moved by the boy's innocence. The boy needed oxygen and dry land to survive. But he was willing to leave the safety of everything else for the safety of his father. And even if it turned out to be the wrong choice, death with someone he loved was preferable to survival alone.

When the man pushed from shore, he had the boy's body-weight to maneuver as well. They surged downstream. The man dogpaddled, but that did nothing. They hit a rock, and the man was able to push off. The boy grabbed him around the neck, which made the man's face submerge. For several seconds, he had to fight his own son to breathe. Then he got his face above the surface again.

"I can't get us across alone," the man said. "We both need to swim."

"But you won't let go?"

"I won't let go."

"We'll stay together?"

"We'll stay together."

The man held the boy with one hand and swam with his other. The boy began to paddle on his own. The river was still carrying them farther and farther downstream. But now they were able to get closer to the other side. Once, the man lost his grip on the boy's torso. They both clambered for each other and then floated, doing nothing but hugging in the current. After a moment, they resumed making their way across.

Once they were on land, the man looked back. Only now that it was over could he see how dangerous what he'd just done was.

They'd been carried several hundred yards downriver, and they had to walk back to their stuff naked and shivering. Tree branches snagged on their skin. Debris cut their feet. Once they'd retrieved their packs, they yanked on their clothes, exhaling in relief. They were out of time now. They both knew it, and they rushed off.

They moved quickly, each on the threshold of panic, their fear driving them faster and faster until they were crashing through the forest. Once, the boy stumbled, and the man hauled him to his feet.

An echo carried in the distance, the etched sound of wood smashing.

The man never glanced back. With the boy by his side, he kept scrambling forward, not liking the sound and trying to keep ahead of whatever it was. When the sound repeated, the man realized it was getting closer.

It gained on them, growing louder and louder. Suddenly there was crashing so close it pulsed across the man's skin. He grabbed the boy and froze as the sound overtook them.

Deer exploded from the trees, springing in every direction.

The boy let out a gasp. Several zigzagged, almost colliding with them. The man could feel the fear running through their hides. They were fleeing something. And once he and the boy were able to move again, he kept looking back in the direction the deer had come from.

Thunder sounded far away, quiet yet gigantic, a whisper from something enormous.

Another thunderclap. This one so close it shook the air in the back of the man's throat.

The rain began with sudden force. Like it had been waiting above them, suspended, this entire time. The boy murmured but never stopped moving. When they reached the side of the mountain, they found a rock that jutted out forming an over-hang, and they huddled together underneath.

The rain fell in heavy, high-velocity sheets. When the man put his arm out, the droplets almost hurt his hand. The wind was what frightened him though. There'd be a gust, and an entire section of the forest momentarily disappeared. Hun-dred-year-old trees would be bent in half. And when the wind subsided, they continued to slump as if their spines had been broken.

The wind kept picking up.

It was already so strong the man could barely stand it. But soon the gusts began to spin the air, kicking dirt into their cringing faces. The man and the boy clung to each other, and they were nothing but two pairs of eyes watching and waiting.

In the distance, there was a sound like a freight train. The man listened as the sound came closer. Soon the trees began to bend in one direction, then the opposite. The man felt himself and the boy being pulled from the cave. The boy cried out, and the man grabbed him and jammed his free hand into crags in

57

the rock.

They never saw what had created the sound. It remained just out of sight. But even from a distance, they could feel its presence, a monster traveling through the forest on its way to destroy something—anything—else.

CHAPTER

THE STORM'S full force had come and gone. It was still raining and gusting, but the man and the boy ventured out and continued north. The man watched the boy as they walked. By the man's count, the boy had a week, maybe two, before absolutely anything could happen to his body.

The boy began to laugh. "It's kind of funny," he said. "We really could die out here."

"We really could."

"But I don't mind."

Now the man cracked a smile.

"If people were watching us in a movie," the boy said, "they'd be like, *What the hell are they doing? Go home.* But I don't want to go home."

"Me either. I'm enjoying our vacation from reason and common sense."

The boy laughed, which made the man laugh.

"I've been reflecting on my behavior over the last two days," the man said. "And I have to be honest. I think I've lost my goddamn mind, but you know what?"

"What?"

"I'm loving every minute of it."

They both huddled under some trees to rest and be out of the rain.

"I feel like I *should* be more scared," the boy said. "But I can't figure out why I'm not."

"We've gone over the edge."

"What do you mean?"

"You spend your whole life scared of going over the edge. Then one day you get pulled over it. Suddenly you're right there—with everything you always feared. And you realize it's not so bad once you stop caring so much and you just let go."

"What do they call it when you're facing death and stuff, yet it makes you laugh?"

"Gallows humor."

"Why would being hanged make someone laugh?"

"Because something in you just says, *Fuck it.*"

The boy nodded. "I like that. Fuck it."

"Something in you says, *You know what? It was all just a game. So what do you do when the whole thing is meaningless and rigged? You let your spirit out for a romp, and you play the most magnificent fucking game there is."*

A grin came across the boy's face. "You have more gallows humor than anyone I know, Dad."

The man grinned back. "Fuck yeah I do."

They both laughed.

The boy looked off, then back at his dad. "But you know what I think? Something must have made you that way."

The man stared at his dying child. "A lot of things made me that way."

The boy said nothing.

"You have gallows humor too," the man said.

"I do?"

"Yeah. It's one of my favorite things about you."

The boy looked sad, then seemed to will it away. "I meant what I said earlier," he said, his voice catching. "For right now, I'm not scared to die."

"If it meant you could live, I'd stay with you here forever."

"What about Mom and Sid?"

"They're so far away right now. It all is."

They were both silent.

"Sometimes I wish I could just die with you," the man said.

The boy stiffened, like something powerful was surging through him. And when he spoke, it was through miles of depth, miles of feeling. "We'll never see each other again, will we?"

The man said nothing.

"I'm going to be alone."

"No, I'll be with you."

"But after. I'll be alone right after."

Once again the man said nothing.

The boy thought a moment. "I saw a movie once where a man died, and he could still hear his daughter talking to him. Then suddenly he was in a forest, and everything was different. A man told him to come with him, and he had no choice. He had to go." The boy looked over. "You won't be able to protect me when I'm dead, will you?"

The man watched his son. Then he grabbed the boy and hugged him violently. "I don't know. God, I just don't know."

Afterward there was a silence, one the man wished would never end. Then they got up and kept moving.

CHAPTER

THE FARTHER the man and the boy pushed north, the more their trip changed.

Montana was already itself an outpost, but soon they seemed to be separated from the rest of the world not just by distance but by something else. And they began to see things far stranger than anything the man ever had before.

They passed the skeleton of an enormous caribou. A hole had been caved into the side of its ribcage where something had burst out. They passed a deer that just won in mortal combat against another buck. The other buck's head had been severed and its antlers had caught on the victor's. Now the dead creature's head dangled down, and the two deer—one living, one dead—traversed the forest stuck face-to-face.

The man and the boy passed ravines and caves and other holes in the world where probably not a single person had ever been. They found an old cabin abandoned decades ago.

Everything was still inside: cereal boxes from the 80s, a Walkman, even a rifle. The place had been someone's home for years. Now it was just yet another corpse.

They passed areas that were so silent it was as though everything, even time, had stopped. In the end, they passed through the greatest emptiness, the greatest wilderness, the man had ever known. And the man and the boy were just two small afterthoughts, two things too small to destroy, picking their way across a planet too vast to know they were even there.

And as the man looked out over the brute, wondrous, terrible immensity of Montana, he was leveled by a thought. Everyone, everything, was marked for death. And not only would that never change, but nothing about life had ever changed. They said science and technology would one day perform the miracles that gods once had. They said that one day they'd cure every illness, answer every question and make the species immortal. And the man saw how deranged and laughable that was. Nothing people did would ever lead them to anything different or better, just to more of the same.

One of the most haunting concepts he'd ever come across was Nietzsche's eternal recurrence. Eternal recurrence was the idea that because time was infinite and the physical world was finite, the same events had to recur over and over—forever. But even Nietzsche hadn't taken this concept all the way to its pale dead end. Recurrence meant there was no escape from the past—because the future would be just like it. It meant there was nothing new or different. And no one was unique or special. Billions of other people had already thought your thoughts and dreamed your dreams. Meanwhile there was no hope of change across the ages. Instead each generation was destined to repeat the struggles of the ones that came before it. And you couldn't escape—though you'd try. Everyone tried.

The man looked out. A hundred years ago, a thousand, a man and his son had likely stood exactly where they were now. And they'd felt the same pain and been shackled to the same fate that his and his own son were.

The man remembered when the boy, just five, had first learned that someday he'd die. Here was this little creature that had just become aware of itself. And then it discovered that one day it'd all end. The boy looked at his father, his eyes full of a child's faith in decency and justice, as if to say, *How could something so terrible be true?*

And the man thought that's what life is: to want what is impossible for you to have. Meanwhile even if you got everything you wanted, even if you had a thousand lives, you'd make all the same mistakes, return to all the same points. The man thought of all the people who'd died before him: all those crushed hopes, all those boulevards of broken dreams. He thought of how fatherhood had brought him here, how it had destroyed him. He thought of how he'd once been a writer, and that had destroyed him too. And he realized it was the most worthwhile things that killed you. Because the more you lived, the more you loved something, the more you could die.

In a few weeks, he'd experience the most complete destruction there was. He looked at his son. Only when you got close enough, only when you truly saw it, could you understand how incredible something was—and how it didn't belong to anyone. It hadn't even belonged to itself.

They walked for several days. And for several days, the man was barely able to speak. The man's dreaminess evaporated, though, the instant they found bear sign.

Bear scat dotted the side of the path. Beside it were the remains of an animal too destroyed to be identified.

"How old do you think this is?" the boy asked.

"Not that old. Maybe a week."

There was a place both deep inside a person and far, far away. It was there that words ended and something else began. When the man and the boy reached the Voreland Gate, they also reached that place.

Both fell silent in awe.

The rock formed a gigantic circular portal, one that didn't look natural, yet clearly wasn't man-made. Instead it seemed inhuman, like something carved in another age by an alien race.

As they passed through, something paled inside the man. He reached out and touched the boy as if to confirm him in some way.

They were now in the Cauldron.

The change in atmosphere was immediate. The up-country here had an eeriness so overpowering it made the man's skin crawl. Trees obscured the sky, and even the daylight felt dark. It truly was as the hunters had described, and he marveled that their exaggerations were no such thing. This was what existed once you'd gone past laws and countries, past everything towering and solid upon which all human life relied. Once, it had been called the frontier. But really it was the nameless place the Indians referred to when they spoke of God and ancient spirits and things like the wendigo, the flesh-eater that looked like a man and waited in the farthest woods with its wide, shiny eyes.

They found more bear sign.

Fresher than what they'd found earlier.

The man stood surveying the landscape. Somewhere out there was the serial killer they'd traveled two thousand miles to find.

That night, strange noises trickled in from the woods. The man kept hearing what sounded like a woman's voice. It was soft and clipped, like he was catching a stray word in the middle of a conversation.

In the morning, every time the man and the boy heard a sound, they shouldered their rifles and waited for something to materialize out of the murk. The terrain added to their unease. It wasn't wide-open like the rest of Montana. Instead they were in a maze of trees where something could be twenty feet away yet entirely invisible. The result was a suffocating feeling of blindness. This was a forest that trapped you in with whatever else was in there.

They kept moving north toward the Crossing.

"I don't know if this is a good idea," the man said.

"It probably isn't." The boy sounded so reasonable it surprised the man.

"It's funny. It actually feels like something's out there."

"I feel it too." The boy had an adult, almost parental look on his face. "I'm a little worried. I don't want anything to happen to you, Dad."

"To me?" The man almost laughed. "Don't worry about me."

"Well, I've been thinking about it. We don't each stand to

lose the same thing."

"How's that?"

"I only have a few weeks, but you have years. I can see why you'd be more scared."

The man laughed again. "So you're both concerned about me, and you're calling me a chicken shit. Do I have that right, you little bastard?"

The boy grinned. "No, I really mean it."

"Can I you tell you something? It doesn't work like that."

"What doesn't work like that?"

"A parent will die to protect a child, but not vice versa. A child should never die to protect a parent."

"Why?"

"Because you're the future. You're our only chance."

"Only chance to do what?"

"To keep going. To maybe finally get it right."

The boy thought a moment. "But I'm not the future."

"The principle still holds. Your life is still more important than mine."

"But you still have to be a dad to Sidney. I should protect you, so you can be that to her."

The man looked at his son and for a moment was unable to speak.

He leaned down close to the boy. "I want to talk to you

about something."

"Okay."

"In a month, you'll be dead. I don't know it for sure, but it's my hope that we all have souls. Do you understand what that is?"

The boy nodded, but the man could tell he didn't understand.

"Do you know why I'm here?" the man asked.

"You wanted to do one last nice thing for me?"

"Yes, but what I really want is for you to have lived. For you to have gone to the places you always thought were out there. But most of all I want for this right here"—he touched the boy's chest—"to grow as much as possible before you die."

"But what if I don't have a soul? Then it'll all be for nothing."

"Is there anything else that seems more important or more interesting to you than what I've just described?"

"No."

"Then even if it's for nothing, it isn't for nothing."

They were both quiet for a moment.

Then the man said, "And let me tell you another thing. Even if you mean nothing to this world, you're not nothing to me."

"But what if you don't have a soul either?" the boy asked. "What if you're nothing too?"

"Then fuck it. We'll be nothing together."

As they walked, every so often they'd find an excuse to

touch each other. The man would tousle the boy's hair. The boy would pat his father's back.

"I'm proud of you, you know that?" the man said.

"Why?"

"You should see yourself holding that rifle."

"What's so great about that?"

"You're facing the worst thing a person can. Life ripped out your heart and handed it back to you. Yet you're still trying. You're still ready to drop the hammer." The man paused, his voice catching. "Bravest goddamn thing I've ever seen."

The boy said nothing, but his expression spoke for him. The man didn't think he'd ever seen someone more honored in his life.

That night, as the boy slept, the man heard crashing through the forest. Something large moved faster in total darkness than any person could in daylight. The woods became silent again. Then he heard what sounded like a woman screaming. The distance made it faint. He remembered that a fox's howl could sound like a woman being attacked. There were stories of people getting lost in the woods, trying to stop what they thought was a murder.

A twig snapped.

It was outside the glow of the fire but within the perimeter of the camp. The man grabbed his rifle, racked it. He stared in the direction of the sound.

Another twig snapped.

Behind him this time.

The man turned, scanning the forest, watching the darkness between the trees, wondering what if anything was staring back. He stayed like that for half an hour, absolutely sure that something was there. Then he grew tired—both of being awake and of his fear.

In the morning, he searched around the camp and found nothing. No droppings. No prints. He and the boy ate breakfast and then kept going. They'd only gone several miles when they found a tree trunk scratched bare. Later, they found prints around a stream. The man put his boot in one of the prints. It was like a toddler putting its hand inside an adult's.

"How much bigger is it than you, Dad?"

The man calculated. "Probably five times."

"I didn't know they got that big." The boy stared off. "God, it's like something out of the Ice Age."

"When it's on all fours, its shoulders come up to my face."

"Do you think this is the one?"

"Don't know. But we don't want to face him in this forest. He has the advantage here."

"Why?"

"The trees. Our strategy is to shoot him from far away. But his strategy is to get up nice and close. The trees make it so we can't even see fifty yards ahead. That's why he uses the Cauldron as a hunting ground. It handicaps his prey."

The man looked around. "This forest is a giant labyrinth, and he's the monster waiting at the end."

They walked another day, finding more and more sign. They were just fifteen miles from Skinner's Crossing, the most active sector of the hunting ground, the place where years ago some people had built a town. They hiked up a small rise, and as they went down the other side, the man grabbed the boy and hauled him back the way they came.

The boy, who'd seen what the man had seen, was mute. They'd almost walked right into it. Thirty yards away, the biggest grizzly the man had ever laid eyes on was pulling a root out of the ground. The man wasn't sure if it had seen them, but it'd pick up their scent soon, if it hadn't already.

They retreated farther and then crept around to the animal's flank. From higher ground, they could see it up close through the scopes of their rifles. The man took out the picture of the bear they'd been given back in camp. It had a massive white stripe across his back.

He put his eye back on the scope. "It isn't him."

"How do you know?"

"This one doesn't have the stripe."

"We've come so far. Should we shoot it anyway?"

The man turned.

The boy grinned. "I'm just kidding."

"I don't like this," the man said. "We're going north to the Crossing. These bears also seem to be going north to the Crossing. Which means we have some of them ahead we'll stumble into and some coming up behind while our backs are turned."

The boy thought a moment. "Yeah, but that increases the chances of finding our bear."

"Well, yes, there's that. But there's also not having the largest American land carnivore chew off my penis while I'm still alive."

The boy burst out laughing. Then he said, "Did you know lizards can regrow their penises?"

"No, but I've never liked lizards, and somehow that doesn't surprise me."

"Well, they can."

"But that begs the question."

"What question?"

The man bent down. "Why in the name of god are the lizards' penises coming off in the first place?"

The boy was laughing so hard now he couldn't breathe.

"I mean, where are they sticking these things?" the man asked. "Also of interest, why haven't they learned to stop?"

"Dad, they're lizards. They just, you know, live."

"Yeah, a little too freely, I'd say."

They continued north, and the man kept looking behind them. He wondered if he was leading his son into the same trap that killed a town of people years ago.

They made camp that night and sat talking about how scared they'd been when they almost walked into the bear.

The man had brought the boy's favorite hot cocoa, Swiss Miss with extra marshmallows. He made them each a cup.

The boy took a sip and sighed like an adult decompressing after a long day. "This is the stuff."

As the man watched his son, he was amazed at how abruptly a little man had emerged from a child. Three years ago, the boy still had stuffed animals. Now he was old enough to kill something.

For some reason, the man remembered the night before his son's sixth birthday. He'd woken the boy in the middle of the night.

"Hi, Dad," the boy had said, groggy.

"I just wanted to give you one last hug as a five-year-old."

The boy never turned down a hug and on reflex opened his arms.

"I had so much fun this past year with the five-year-old you," the man said. "And I just realized that child will never exist again."

"But I'll still be alive."

"Yes, but as something different."

"It's still me."

"It is. But when you move forward, some part of you has to be left behind." The man smiled. "I don't know if that makes any goddamn sense."

"Dad, why are you so sad sometimes?"

"I don't know. Go back to bed. I'm just a crazy old man."

The campfire had burned low, and the boy was asleep.

The man looked around their campsite. It was this little island of light and warmth against endless darkness. He didn't want to leave. Didn't want this moment to end. He wished he could stay here, suspended, until something out there discovered he'd cheated time and reversed the error.

He thought of his house two thousand miles away.

When he'd work from home, there were times when the house was empty. He'd be enjoying the peace and quiet. Then he'd go downstairs. The lights would be off. He'd stand there, and for a moment it was like none of them were ever coming back. And he'd stare at the toys no children would ever again play with. The photos of people who no longer mattered to anyone. Outside, the sun shined, and the traffic passed a home where once there'd been so much. In those moments, the man knew what it meant to die. He could feel the silence of it.

And he'd think, *Please bring them back.* He'd picture their faces. There was something so well-meaning in each one. And he'd realize that they were his people. The only people he was ever going to get.

The man shot out of sleep and jerked upright.

He hadn't heard a sound, but he was startled. Or at least he sensed something was about to startle him.

He listened, his heart slamming in his chest. The fire had burned down. He put one hand on his rifle and searched the darkness and all its depths.

Eventually he laid back down. But he couldn't escape the feeling the campsite was no longer theirs.

In the morning, he found bear scat just thirty yards from where he and the boy had slept.

He crouched, thinking.

"What's that?" the boy asked.

77

"A bear came up on us while we were asleep."

The boy's eyes widened with the rustle of pleasure a person gets when the stakes have been finally and irreversibly raised.

"What do we do?" he asked.

"I'm not sure. But we may have found our bear—or he may have found us."

He and the boy continued their trek north. They'd only gone a few hundred yards when they saw the crows. They were pecking and pulling at something. When the man approached, they took off. Blood soaked the ground and stained the carcass's fur, like paint spilled on a stuffed animal.

As the man walked closer, he saw the rest of the body. The boy had appeared at his side, and the man did nothing to shield his eyes. It was the giant grizzly they'd seen the day before. Its head had been torn off.

CHAPTER

THE CROSSING was just ten miles away when they made camp that night. The man and the boy still talked, but now every so often they'd both stop suddenly and listen.

The man watched the sun set. He could see now that a thing was brightest only when it was on the verge of going out. Then darkness set in. His stomach tightened, and he was reminded of how people long ago feared the night. The boy talked of staying up to keep watch. For an hour, he scanned the area more keenly than any adult could. An hour later, he was fast asleep.

The man took a leak and stopped at the exact dividing line between their camp and the wilderness around it. They could be attacked from any side. He didn't want to sleep, but his exhaustion told him that soon he'd have no say in the matter.

He hadn't told the boy how the bear they'd found had been killed—in total silence. There wasn't even a fight. Something had subdued it so completely it hadn't even made a sound.

The man tried to picture such a creature as he drifted off, falling down through miles and miles of thought.

He jerked awake. Once again it was to a sound that hadn't been made.

He surveyed the woods, feeling the forest's pale indifference, its utter lack of mercy or lenience.

A twig snapped.

The man grabbed his rifle. He waited for the sound to repeat. He sat waiting for a long time. Then he couldn't keep his eyes open, and hypotheticals like his death, or his son's death, no longer seemed paramount. As he drifted off, sleep released him from the body that was so tired.

In the morning, the man was surprised he and the boy were okay. He checked the perimeter of camp and froze when he saw the prints. He put his foot inside one. It was larger than the print he and his son had found two days earlier.

He woke the boy. "We need to leave."

"Why?"

"Because the thing we're hunting is now hunting us."

The boy gathered his things. "What do we do?"

"Fall back."

"Isn't this maybe a good thing?"

The man almost laughed. "How's that?"

"Before, we had to search all over to find him. But now he's come to us. Can't we just sit back and wait?"

"He's coming at night. That changes everything. We can't ambush him, but pretty much anything he does is an ambush on us."

The woods had always been eerie, but they looked different now that they were the ones being tracked. The man knew that grizzlies usually weren't nocturnal. As they walked back, he kept turning and scanning the maze of trees, waiting for something's face to appear.

That night, the boy wanted to stay awake with him, but the man insisted that one of them rest. And he realized that he'd stopped seeing his son as a sick child. Now the boy was a junior partner who needed to pull his weight.

The boy loved that. It made him swell with determination.

The man watched him as he slept. He leaned over and ran his hand through the boy's damp hair.

The man woke to the twig-breaking sound.

He turned on his phone to check the time, hoping it was close to dawn. But it was only midnight.

He heard another twig break.

The forest had gone silent.

The man reached for his rifle and nudged the boy. "It's here."

The boy showed no surprise. He grabbed his weapon and scanned for targets like he'd been waiting for this moment his entire life.

Wind gusted through the trees, so loud it imposed a kind of deafness. The man touched the ground. He could feel the vibration of footsteps. He and the boy trained their rifles ahead. They did it with every fiber of their being pouring out their hearts and down the barrel of their guns. And in that moment, no object had ever been an extension of the man's body more than his rifle.

They waited and waited, but nothing happened. The man clicked on his flashlight.

Something moved suddenly off to the side.

But when he swung the light around, there was just a branch swaying like something heavy had brushed it. The man spun around and shined the light behind them. He kept turning in a circle, but it was impossible. An attack could occur from anywhere.

"We have to get out of here," the man said.

"Where can we go?"

"Those rocks. We have to get someplace it can't attack us from behind."

They left their packs and rushed through the forest. Running made everything worse. Their panic fed back on itself, amplifying, until they were panicking that they were panicking.

The man grabbed his son to slow him. "This is the time to keep our wits."

The man covered one flank, and the boy covered the other.

Suddenly there was the sound of something massive crashing through the forest. Both their instincts were to run, but the man looked at the boy and shouldered his rifle. The boy did the same. They turned to face whatever was coming.

The crashing sound ricocheted off the trees, multiplying.

The man reached out and touched his son. Once he'd confirmed where the boy was, he knew the only area he had to defend in absolute. The sound got closer. Terror tightened the man's throat. Yet it was an incredible terror. A terror that expanded him. There were no more theoreticals now, only what would happen. They were at that place where talk ended, and something far more important began.

A shape was moving in their direction.

The man fired.

A hulking silhouette rose up before him. He fired again. Something hit the man in the chest. As he fell, he reached for the boy but felt nothing. The man collided with the ground and bolted upright, aiming the rifle. He made out the tiny outline of the boy. Refusing to flee, the boy took aim and began to fire point-blank. He got off two shots. Then something hit the boy so hard the man was sure the life had been knocked out of him.

The boy's body was motionless on the ground for a second. Then the body disappeared, and the boy began to shout in terror.

He was being dragged off.

Half-blind in the darkness, the man ran in the direction of the sound, firing into the air. When he found the boy, the boy's jacket had been ripped apart, but somehow he was okay. They hurried to the rock and laid down under its scant protection, holding each other. When morning came, the man couldn't believe they were still alive.

CHAPTER

THE BOY had scratches, but the teeth marks had barely broken the skin. The man looked himself over. He had three rows of lacerations on his arm and a giant bruise on his chest. He almost couldn't believe their shit luck.

"I peed myself," the boy said.

"I don't think I'll relax enough to pee ever again."

Each looked more closely at the condition of the other, and they started to laugh.

"If your mother could see us now..." the man said.

"She'd *murder* us."

"Our only chance would be to shoot her and the bear."

Soon they were laughing so hard neither could speak.

They'd left their packs at camp, and they patrolled their way back, rifles ready. When they reached the campsite, nothing had been touched. The packs were just as they'd left them. It looked like the scene of an unsolved mystery.

They gathered their things, and as they left, it occurred to the man that they'd never even seen the bear.

They needed new clothes, and they needed rest, so they headed toward Hanover, the town they'd been told to go to in an emergency.

They were close to the Voreland Gate when the boy stopped. "What are we going to do once we get there?"

"Thank our lucky stars we still have eyes, ears and mostly functional penises."

When the boy didn't laugh at the last part, the man suddenly remembered that the boy would never have a child of his own. Never know what it was like to be with a woman.

"I think it's time to head home," the man said.

The boy's eyes were wide, intense—the way they got when his mind was running its relentless little algorithms. "I don't want to go home yet."

The man said nothing.

"I'm not ready—for what's back there."

"We don't know how much time we have. You really don't want to go home?"

"No, do you?"

The man was quiet for a moment. "No, it almost feels like there's nothing for me back there."

"Dad, please don't say that."

"I just don't want this to end."

"Me either."

The boy leaned his head against the man, and the man put his arm over the boy. They walked that way for a bit.

"Is it possible to stay?" the boy asked, trying to be nonchalant.

"I'm not sure."

"We won't get into trouble or anything?"

"No, we're past all that. There's no one here, and there probably never will be."

"How far is that town?" the boy asked.

"Fifteen miles."

"Okay."

They had to stop midway to make camp. As they sat by the fire, they told stories of each other's bravery under fire. Then it was time for bed. The boy laid down. Now that they were no longer looking at each other, the boy was able to broach what had been on his mind.

"I'd like to go back for that bear."

The man said nothing.

"I think we could get it. I really think we could."

"That thing isn't like anything I've ever heard of. It had this…terrible intelligence."

87

"We just weren't prepared. But we will be next time."

"Your mother has been saying this for years, and I always dismissed it, but she's right. You really are a dog with a bone."

The boy's eyes were closed. He chuckled. "Thank you."

CHAPTER

WHEN THE TOWN APPEARED, its normalcy made it seem like a mirage. Along with a few houses, there was a gas station, a diner and a motel. That was it. They hiked down, took off their packs and walked into the diner.

There was an assortment of ranchers and backwoods types.

The man could only imagine what sort of impression the two of them made with their ripped clothes and filthy faces.

An old-timer turned and froze. "What in the blue fuck ate you two and shat you out?"

"The Voreland Gate."

The old man nodded, impressed. "What brought you up there?"

"The bear hunt."

The old man nodded again. Then he looked at the boy. "How old are you?"

"Ten."

"You got stones, kid. Shit."

"Language, Ed," an older waitress said.

"Sorry, Darlene." The old man winked at them. "That's my wife."

The waitress came over and offered them a booth. She paused when she saw the state of their clothes. "How is it out there?"

"It's been a very exciting, very heart-stopping vacation."

Some of the other diners laughed.

"You see the bear?" the old-timer asked. And the others gave him looks as though he'd been rude.

"We saw something."

"Did that something do that to your clothes?"

"It did." The man checked the menu, then looked back up. "There a place here we can get new stuff?"

"There's a lost and found at the motel." The old-timer winked. "It's a regular secondhand store, and the price is right."

"Thank you."

Several patrons paid and walked out. It was late afternoon. Lunch was over, and the people who remained seemed to be regulars who never left.

"Is this the whole town?" the man asked.

"This is it," the waitress said. "One road in, and one road out. We get snowed in every winter."

"It ever bother you sometimes, being up so far?"

The waitress laughed. But when she saw the man was serious, she became serious as well. "What do you mean? Bother us?"

"It ever scare you a little?"

The old-timer and his wife looked at each other.

"What are you thinking we'd be scared of?" the old-timer asked.

"Of what it's like out there."

The old-timer spoke carefully. "Sure, we get scared."

No one else said anything.

The man and the boy ordered lavish meals, which they polished off in minutes. There was no cell service. So when they were finished, they used an old payphone to call home. The boy's mom answered, and the boy launched into stories about all that they'd done. Afterward the man got on.

"When are you coming back?" his wife asked.

"He doesn't want to come back yet."

The woman fell silent.

"But that would mean there's less time with him for you, maybe none at all," the man said.

"I miss him so much. All I want is to give him a giant hug."

The man nodded.

"But if it's his wish to stay there," the woman continued,

"then who am I to stand in the way?"

"It's funny. That's an almost unthinkable thing for a mother to say, but somehow I knew you'd say that."

"Is he having fun?"

"It's bigger than that. He's on a quest."

"How are you?"

"I suppose I'm on one too."

"You feel so far away."

"I am far away."

"I wish I could see your face."

"I wish I could see yours."

"Listen, if something happens and you don't make it back in time, can you…" She exhaled. "Can you make sure that at the very end his bucket is full?"

"I can try."

"God, I wish I could see your face. I love you."

"I love you too."

They hung up. Dial tone came on. The man stared at the receiver and then put it back in the cradle. Now the connection with everything back home had been severed.

The man booked a room at the motel. He and the boy took showers. The hot water felt so good each couldn't resist narrating its effect on him to the other.

"Oh my god," the man called out as he lathered up. "I'm doing my crotch now. I wish you could smell this."

"Thanks, but I prefer to live."

The boy began to grow suspicious.

"Are you bending over and washing your ass?"

"Vigorously."

The boy made a vomiting sound. He'd always found this practice of his father's particularly distasteful.

"I just cracked my cheeks," the man called out cheerfully. "Now I'm rinsing, and my god you should see what's coming out of there. I feel like Hercules cleaning the Augean stables."

The boy collapsed outside the bathroom and pretended to gag to death.

When they switched places, the boy exhaled with relief the way his father had.

"How's it going?" the man asked as he toweled off.

"Oh my lord."

"That good?"

"Do you want to know how good this feels?"

"Hell yeah I do."

Grinning, the boy leaned out of the shower and motioned for his dad. Then he put his mouth against the man's ear and whispered, *My balls are tingling.*

At dinnertime, they went back to the diner. The man let the boy order everything he wanted, so the boy ordered waffles, a banana sundae, an elk burger, chocolate cake and a hot dog with relish and beer cheese.

"What's the special occasion?" the waitress asked.

"My son just became a hunter."

A trucker glanced over. "What do you hunt?"

Some of the regulars turned, interested.

The old-timer they'd spoken to earlier answered for the boy. "He's been hunting bear."

"But what have you killed?" the trucker asked.

"I killed a gopher." The boy thought a moment. "I could have killed a bear. Also a moose. But it was the wrong bear, and we wouldn't have eaten the moose, so I didn't."

"So you kill only when you have to?"

"I've never had to. Only when it's worth something, I suppose."

"Well, you sound like a hunter to me."

"I'll tell you something else," the boy said, excited. "That bear that ripped up our clothes, I fired at him point-blank."

"You hit him?" the old-timer asked.

The boy grinned. "Nah."

The old-timer turned to the waitress. "Will you get the bottle please, Darlene?"

When she brought out a green bottle of dark liquid, the old-timer uncorked it and poured some into glasses for everyone there. Someone handed a glass to the man.

The old-timer held his glass up. "When someone has a good hunt, we sometimes drink this stuff."

"What is it?" the boy asked.

"Whiskey."

"Can I have one too?"

The old-timer looked at the man and raised his eyebrows. The man nodded, and soon the boy had his own glass in front of him.

"Kid, you may have only killed one gopher. But anyone who fires at a bear point-blank is a true-blue hunter to me."

The adults all drank. The boy watched them, then tried the same thing. His body immediately seized. He then proceeded to projectile-vomit across the table.

Everyone in the diner burst out laughing.

Soon the boy was laughing too.

"That's the most honest reaction to whiskey I've ever seen," Darlene said. She helped the man clean up.

"Can I have another one?" the boy asked.

"Another one?" the trucker said.

"I can handle it. I just wasn't ready the first time."

"I don't know," the man said to his son. "You've already had one drink. That's like six drinks for a kid your age."

"Technically," the old-timer said, "he hasn't had anything to drink because, as far as I can see, he didn't keep any of the first one down."

The man exhaled. "Ah, screw it."

Everyone cheered.

The boy got his second drink. All eyes were on him. He took a sip. For a second, his eyes fluttered like he was fighting off a demonic possession. But then he swallowed the whiskey and kept it down.

Everyone cheered again.

"Kid, you got sand," the trucker said. "I'll tell you what. You make it back here next year for elk season, and you can be my right-hand man."

The boy paused a second, then smiled. "I'd like that."

It was late. Everyone had left except for the old-timer and Darlene, who was in the back closing up.

The boy slept against the table. The beer he'd tried to finish sat next to his small fist. He was a terminally ill child who wouldn't survive the month. Yet an hour earlier he'd been drunk and content. It amazed the man. The only way to be alive was to forget what you really were.

The old-timer had moved into the booth with him. They'd

kept drinking and talking long after the others had gone home.

"You don't seem like you're from these parts," the old-timer said. "But I can tell you like it here."

"I do."

"You figured out why?"

"This is the end of the line. Out here, you're past everything. You're the farthest a person can go."

"That's why I came. The rest of it just stopped seeming true to me."

"What stopped seeming true?"

"The grind. The sacrifice for things no one can explain. But here, there's no program to follow. There isn't anything. And I fucking love that."

The man had noticed something out the window. "What's that building over there? Looks like a schoolhouse."

"It was."

The man could tell he'd upset the old-timer. "I didn't mean to pry."

"No, it's okay. Years ago the town was bigger and actually needed a school. It was just like in the prairie days. Kindergarten through sixth grade all in one room."

"Sounds kind of nice."

"It was." The old man nodded. "It was."

Neither spoke for a moment. The boy murmured in his

sleep.

"There was a blizzard," the old-timer said. "Hit out of the blue. A lot of the parents were out at work. Barely had time to shelter themselves. The teacher and the children hunkered down in the school. No one's sure what happened, but we think the power went out, and she decided to try for the diner." The old man shook his head. "Well, the visibility wasn't even a foot. And in a storm, you lose all sense of direction. They only needed to go fifty yards, but they missed the diner, probably by only a few feet. We found their bodies in the commons over there. They died right in the middle of town, but they died lost. As lost as people can be."

The old man took a breath.

"Anyway they called it the Children's Blizzard," he said. "That storm was theirs, and they were its."

"I don't know how a place recovers from something like that."

"The town was a very sad place for a time. But it's funny how those things work. The parents all left, and new people came in. They learned of the storm, but it was different for them. That's how it goes with everything, I suppose. People never change. They're just replaced by different people."

The old man thought a moment. "I guess nothing really ever changes. It just seems like it does because it gets forgotten."

"I hope you don't mind me saying, but it sounds like you had a child in that school."

"Me? No. But I said hi to them every day. They were—well, they were just like kids."

The old-timer pointed at the sleeping boy. "What about your little man over there?"

The man stared at his son.

"Unusual trip for a boy that age," the old man said.

"He's dying."

The old man became very still. Finally he looked at the man and said, "I'm sorry."

The man nodded.

"It's interesting," the old man said, and his voice was sad. "I know people who have everything. They're wealthy, beautiful. They have it as easy as a person can. Yet they're married to someone who doesn't love them, or because their lives are so easy, they never got to be anything. It really is amazing. Every life, in a very real sense, is a tragedy. And no one wins. No one gets away. You can never get life at a discount to what it must be paid."

A song came on the radio. The man and the old-timer stared out the window together.

"It's nice being here, isn't it?" the old-timer said.

"It is."

A silence.

"I wish I could stay in this moment forever."

The old man glanced at the boy. "I wish you could too."

The man stayed until he could no longer keep his eyes open. He paid the check and picked up his son. Outside the diner, the man turned with the boy in his arms. The lights from the building barely penetrated the ocean of darkness. It was like mankind's last outpost. And for a moment, the man didn't want to leave the warmth of its glow.

The old man was still sitting by himself in the empty diner. He sat like he would be there forever, and somehow the man was grateful for that.

And as the man stood there, he realized he didn't know anything anymore. He didn't know what to believe in or what good cause he ought to serve. He was beyond everything he'd ever known. And he'd been laid bare. Stripped of every conceit, every fiction, of everything he desperately wished was true. And whatever was left over in a person after that, that was what he had become.

CHAPTER

THE MAN AND THE BOY spent the night in the motel. The next morning, they found new coats in the lost and found. Then they took one last meal in the diner. Everyone asked the boy what his first hangover was like. Then they asked about his plans for the bear. The old-timer handed the man something and whispered in his ear. And when the man and the boy left to go back up into the hills, all the regulars said goodbye and wished them luck.

As the two of them walked to the Voreland Gate, the man felt himself being pulled back into something powerful. He could tell the boy felt it too. And he was aware that he was offering both himself and his son up to something larger and older than they were. He knew the danger. He also knew it could be no other way. This was a game in which you bet yourself. And like all who made that wager, like warriors, sportsmen, like all risk-takers, they did something that wasn't strictly necessary.

And yet it had to happen. Something deep in the human soul needed the highest victory which required the highest stakes.

For a moment, the man was struck by the giganticness of it. And then he understood the horrifying truth. It was only when he wagered his life that he realized how much he loved it.

When they reached the Voreland Gate, they both stopped. The eerie formation stood up above them, just as magical and brutal as before.

They passed through, and then they were in the Cauldron. Now that they were back in the dark wood, the man felt the same fear he had the first time. But it was a good fear, one that reminded you that you were living on nothing but your wits and you weren't supposed to make it. It was just you and your self-belief against an entire world.

They returned to the site where the bear had almost killed them.

Blood stained the ground, some of it the bear's, some of it theirs. The man knelt, thinking. The bear had been moving north when they'd intercepted it. Probably it had continued moving north.

They hiked in that direction, searching for bear sign. The man didn't know whether he and the boy would succeed or fail. But he felt the destiny the boy had spoken of when they first arrived. It was here that, one way or another, they would meet their fate.

That night, they climbed a giant ridge. At the top, they were above everything for miles and miles. It was like they stood at the axis of the continental divide, the precise meridian of planet earth.

They sat side by side, watching the world below. A thunderstorm had formed to the west. Lightning hit the ground, and thunder overlapped like fusillades of artillery. The storm expanded in their direction. It was like glimpsing a theater of war. And for a moment, the man could almost believe that things like death and destruction would never reach them.

"Look." The boy pointed at the plains in the distance.

A small herd of buffalo fled the storm, charging across the flat. The boy, like all boys, was obsessed with buffalo. He watched them with concern.

What amazed the man was that the buffalo weren't actually running away from anything. There was no place to run. The storm was already everywhere. And only up here could you see that it was all in vain.

They made camp under pine trees whose limbs formed a roof. They both marveled at how this accidental configuration could keep them perfectly dry as they ate their dinner.

"When were you the happiest?" the boy asked.

"What do you mean?"

"In your life."

"Like was I happiest as a kid or as an adult?"

"Yeah."

"I definitely like being an adult more than being a kid."

"Same."

"You haven't been an adult yet."

"Yeah, but I can tell."

"I don't know that one part of my adulthood was better than the others. The part that meant the most was being a father."

"Really?"

"Yeah."

"Why?"

"Because it's the most important thing you'll ever do. You'll never mean that much to anyone ever again."

The boy said nothing.

The man grinned. "Do you remember a few years ago when you had that giant poop that wouldn't come out?"

"That was worse than breaking my arm."

"You were so scared. The suppository didn't work, so I put Vaseline on my finger and massaged your butt. Most people would have been disgusted, but I loved it. Honestly I was having a whale of a time."

The boy laughed.

"And you were so grateful," the man continued. "No one in my life has ever looked at me the way you did."

"But weren't you happier when you were young and got to do stuff with your friends?"

"I loved that time in my life. It was fun, but fun isn't enough."

"Why not?"

"Because you want there to be something more."

"Like what?"

"You believe there's good in you, and you want the good in you to stand for something."

"Do you know what the good thing in you is?"

"No." The man spoke in a whisper. "I just pray that it's there."

The boy said nothing. He seemed confused, yet also like he was discovering something. The boy stayed that way, a searching expression on his face, until it was time to go to sleep.

"What kind of adult do you think I'd be?" the boy asked.

"I think you'd want to run things."

"I don't like anyone telling me what to do."

"I think you'd maybe start a business, and you'd marry a nice woman."

"I could marry a boy."

"You could. But you wouldn't just be playing video games and eating junk food together. You'd need to kiss him and hold his hand and stuff like that."

"No."

"What?"

"Pass."

"Okay, well, whoever you marry, you're like me. You can only be yourself around someone who goes easy on you."

"Is sex as disgusting as it seems?"

"Yes, and the older I get, the more I enjoy how disgusting it is. In fact I often find it's not disgusting enough."

"Okay. Okay."

The man thought a moment. "I also think you're one of those people who question things, and that would make you lonely."

The boy laid down, but he was still listening.

"I don't think you'd ever find the answers to your questions," the man said. "But my hope is that you'd have friends and a spouse who make you less lonely. And all this sounds kind of sad, but to me it sounds amazing."

"Good night, Dad."

"Good night."

The man woke before the boy. They'd slept up on the ridge. He knew they'd never again come here, so he stared out one last time.

They'd seen things on this trip that he never in his life imagined. But while these things were magical, they weren't enough. In a movie, such things could be the answer all on their own. But in real life, they were just pretty, just poignant bits of scenery. The man had wanted this trip to give them something beyond the existence he'd known so far. He felt that the world he'd known was only a small part of a far larger, far truer one. And somewhere out there was more.

But the more he searched, the less he found.

So what does that leave you?

What does that mean for that boy over there?

Like before, he had no answers. Out of desperation, the man asked himself one final question.

Is there something out there you still know to be true, just one thing?

And he realized there was one last thing in which he still believed. Even if he knew the planet would be blasted to rubble tomorrow, it wouldn't stop him from loving his son. And that was true of everyone. They cared even if it all meant nothing. They kept moving forward even if there was absolutely no point. Religious people called it a person's soul, but there was a silent part within each person that nothing else, not science, not anything, could explain or reach. And whatever could keep going in a person without any love or warmth or encouragement was something the man believed in most of all. This unspoken part was the only thing he knew to be true anymore. It was the only point of any of it. It was the only victory there was.

CHAPTER

THEY MADE THEIR WAY through the Cauldron. They were up near the remote headwaters of Allende Creek, the farthest north they'd ever been. The man could feel the isolation weighing on them, as if it was physically difficult being this far up.

Three days had gone by without bear sign.

The boy vomited one morning.

"I'm okay," he said.

"Do you want anything?"

"I swear I'm okay, Dad."

They got up and started moving again.

"I don't know what to do," the man said. "I think we guessed wrong."

"I think we should keep going."

The boy never looked at his father as he spoke. Instead he looked off, as though he was glimpsing such fleeting things that he couldn't take his eyes off them or they'd be gone forever.

"We don't have a lot of time left," the man said. "I'd hate to waste it."

"This isn't wasting it, not to me. Can we just go a little farther?"

"Of course."

The boy moved closer to the man as they continued walking. "This trip has meant a lot to me. You know why?"

"Why?"

"Because I got to be brave."

"But I've seen you be brave before. At soccer tryouts. When you told that kid who was bullying you to shut up."

"This is different. That was against people."

"And what's this?"

"It's against something bigger."

The man stared at his son. "It would have really been something to see you grow up." His voice was soft. "I'd have loved to see your life."

The boy said nothing.

They continued walking.

After a time, the boy said, "Thank you, Dad."

They'd gone half a day, and the man felt they'd made a terrible mistake. Then the boy called him over and showed him the mound of bear scat.

"He's just eaten a big meal," the boy said. "Look how big that pile of shit is."

The man laughed. "Language please."

"Sorry."

The man knelt down and examined the scat. It was fresh, which meant the bear was close. He checked the map. The bear seemed to be heading in the same direction they were: right toward Skinner's Crossing.

"We're close to that town where all those people died," the man said.

"Can we go there?"

"I don't know if that's a good idea."

"Please."

"Why do you want to see it so much?"

"I don't know. I just do."

They kept going.

"Those people risked a lot," the boy said after a while. "I guess I'm hoping that if we go see it, we'll understand why they wanted to be there so bad."

The landscape flattened and opened up in places. They were able to run spot-and-stalk, the most rigorous type of hunting. Whenever they found high ground, they'd climb up and try to spot the bear, so they could then stalk him. It was the boy who spotted a carcass.

"Dad, look." He pointed to a place a mile away.

They hiked over and found animal remains. The blood was still wet. They continued in the direction the bear seemed to be going. Once again the closeness of the trees gave the man a claustrophobic, blind feeling. Like they were stuck in a labyrinth.

There was also something else. Now that they were only a few miles from the abandoned town, the man had begun to feel its presence. As though it might suddenly appear, before he was ready.

They searched the area and found no sign of the bear. The man knew they had to be running out of time.

"We need to call him," the man said, knowing the danger, wondering whether he'd lost his mind.

They set out bait. The old-timer in Hanover had given the man a bear call. "If you and your boy really want that thing, this might help," the old man had said. "But remember, when you use this, you make yourself the bait."

The man pulled the boy aside. "It's possible he'll come in behind us."

"I'll be careful."

The man used the call until it began to get dark. That was when the bear came.

He and the boy had separated to increase their sight lines. They were still twenty yards apart when the man knelt and touched the ground. Like before, there was no noise, just the vibration of footsteps.

Something nearby exhaled, an enormous sound from enormous lungs.

Then the man finally saw it.

It was walking toward the bait, and its line would bring it right behind the boy. The man trained his rifle on the bear, but the trees blocked his shot. He waited, unable to do anything. The boy had spotted the bear as well. He crept out of its path and hid behind a tree trunk. The man could see the fear almost making him tremble.

When the bear emerged from the trees, it was so large the man thought it couldn't be real. Its shoulders stood six feet off the ground, and its head was the size of an industrial ball bearing. It passed only a few feet from where the boy hid.

The bear could already smell them. Probably it had smelled them a quarter-mile away. And the man thought, *It really no longer has any fear.*

He crept over to the boy. But when he turned, the bear was gone, and so was the bait.

"Where'd it go?"

The man looked in every direction and could see nothing but the maze of trees.

"Use the call, Dad."

The man said nothing.

"If you don't, he'll stalk us again. This way, we're ready."

The boy was right. The man used the call.

Nothing happened.

He used it again.

Immediately they heard footsteps. They both turned, rifles shouldered. The footsteps grew louder. They waited for an impossibly long time for the animal to appear. When the bear burst from the trees, the man fired first.

He couldn't tell whether he'd hit it because it showed no reaction. The boy fired next. The animal flinched, and some remote part of the man's mind felt immense gratitude toward the boy for this.

The bear careened toward them. Both retreated out of its path, still firing. And everything hunters said about hunting bear was true. Its movements so fast and liquid it gave no decent shot presentation. The bear slowed as it turned on them. The man took aim at its chest and fired over and over.

The bear took off, baying, almost screaming.

They ran after it.

When they found the animal, the man put it in his sights. Then he lowered his gun and turned to the boy. "You should do it."

The boy shouldered his rifle, and the massive weapon looked inhuman in his tiny arms. The boy became solemn as he took aim.

The man waited. But the boy never fired.

"Go ahead," the man said. "It's okay."

"Dad, I think he's hurt really bad."

The bear had laid down.

As they walked closer, it only half-watched them.

"Should we shoot him?" the boy asked. "Is he in pain?"

"I don't know. He's lost so much blood." The man poked the bear with his gun. "No, he's past it now."

"Can I touch him?"

"That's not a good idea."

"Please, Dad. I have to."

The man trained his rifle on the animal's face. "Fine, but do it from the back."

The boy went around, looking diminutive beside the bear. He extended his hand. Then he began to stroke its fur.

"What are you doing?"

"I'm helping him pass on."

The man said nothing.

"We watched a video in class. Animals feel less pain when they're being touched." The boy had such an open, youthful look on his face that for a second the man just stared at him.

The bear's breathing had slowed. Its eyes were looking directly at them. The boy moved up to the animal's side. The man started to say something but stopped when the boy began to stroke the bear's head. Its eyes closed for a moment—as if the boy was giving it something it needed to let go.

They stayed with the bear for almost an hour as it died. When it was over, the man touched the boy's shoulder. But neither spoke, as if what had happened was beyond such a thing.

The boy looked at the bear's body and choked something back. "It's funny," he said. "He was a monster, but he was also just a bear."

They walked back to their packs and sat down. The boy frowned as he tried not to cry.

"What is it?" the man asked.

"I was just thinking. God, it'd really be something to spend your life doing stuff like this." The boy looked up. "I love it here. We've done such amazing things. Also it's been nice, just being here with you."

The boy had that open, youthful look again. The man could do nothing but stare at it.

"I've loved it too," the man said. "I don't want it to end."

"It's funny though. We never would have done this unless it was ending."

"No."

"It's terrible that it works like that."

"It is."

The man watched his son. And the man felt perhaps for the first time in his life that he was in the presence of another soul. All the external things about the boy had fallen away. And beneath was the silent, hopeful thing that had always been there.

CHAPTER

THE PAIN started the next day. The boy had a headache.

"Do you want the pills?" the man asked.

"Dad, I'm scared."

"Of what?"

"That it's going to get worse."

"Let's go back."

"I don't want to go back. Not yet."

The man gave him a pill.

They sat waiting for it to work.

"I have a confession," the man said. "I wanted to show you something out here, but I've failed."

"What do you mean? You showed me how to shoot and hunt. You taught me how to survive."

"I thought there'd be something waiting for us at the end of this. Something that would change everything in some way. Change us. But I've realized that's impossible."

"Well, if we failed, at least we failed together," the boy said, smiling.

The pill began to work. Soon the boy was back to normal, talking about caves and whether a polar bear could defeat a grizzly. The man sat watching the boy as he talked. It was amazing what people became when they were entirely unself-conscious.

They ate dinner early. Sometimes they talked, sometimes not. Sometimes the man would lean over and kiss the boy on the top of his head. Other times, he got lost in thought.

The sky turned golden as the sun set. For a moment, the wind stopped. Nothing, not even the animals, made a sound. And it was like the man and the boy were the only two people left in the world. And once they were gone, there'd be no one left.

That night, before they turned in, the boy looked over. "I know I don't have much time, but I'd like to see that town."

"We should get you to a doctor."

"To do what?"

"I don't want you to suffer."

"We have pills, more than I could ever take in a month."

The man rolled onto his back, thinking.

"Will you take me there?" the boy asked.

"I'll take you there."

In the morning, they moved north again. And somehow the man was even more scared than he was when they were hunting the bear. He thought in the days leading up to the boy's death, there'd be endless incredible conversations. But the two of them mostly walked in silence. Before, there'd been urgency to their movement. They were worried they'd run out of time. Now each walked slowly because he knew the town would be the end.

They were only a few hours from the Crossing when they stopped for the evening. The man gathered wood, selecting only the straightest branches. Afterward he made a campfire that looked like something out of a movie. And he realized he'd made it like that because he wanted to remember it this way.

He cooked dinner just how the boy liked it.

"Is it good?" he asked.

"Amazing." The boy looked up. "Can I ask you something?"

"Of course."

"Do you think I'm a good person?"

"Yes."

"You told me once that being good is the most important thing. But most of the time, I don't know if I was good. I was only kind of good."

"Nobody knows."

"But if we're supposed to be good, and we don't even know what that is, isn't that kind of silly? I mean, what's the point?"

"We don't know the point," the man said. "We just hope that there is one."

They each took another bite of food. The light from the campfire kept shifting on their faces.

"Is there really a god?" the boy asked suddenly.

"I don't know."

"If there's a god, maybe there's a heaven."

"That's what they say."

"But you don't believe them?"

"I don't know what to think about anything anymore." And the man knew that was the truest thing he'd ever said in his life.

"I hope there's a heaven," the boy said. "I hope I get in."

Wind gusted through the camp, so loud it silenced them.

"But what if there isn't?" the boy asked.

"Then we just die."

"Is it scary down there?"

It took the man a moment realize what the boy meant. The graves. The boy thought he would be conscious when they put him into the ground with all the others.

"No," the man said, "it's not scary down there."

"Yeah, I'm sure it's not." The boy tried to smile and pretend it wasn't a big deal so he wouldn't worry his dad.

"It's like going to sleep," the man said.

"Do you wish there was a god?"

The man stared at his son who quietly faced unimaginable horror. "If he's a good god, then I hope he's waiting for you. And if he isn't good, then I hope the son-of-a-bitch has accidentally blown himself apart, that or he at least has the decency to leave the rest of us the hell alone after everything he's done."

The boy was quiet a moment. Then he laughed. "Dad, you called God a son-of-a-bitch."

He'd always loved it when his father profaned something sacred. The boy said good night and laid down. The wind began to gust again, and the man stayed up watching his son.

The man sat there for a long time. And he understood there had to be children like this. Only in a random, empty, vicious world could a human life truly stand for something.

The boy would never grow up. Never be more than a boy. His head had been filled with things that were for others, not for him. He wasn't the beneficiary of people's stand against the emptiness. He was the sacrifice that had to be made to it. And that's what the man realized he was looking at: something that had no idea what it was.

CHAPTER

WHEN THEY REACHED the Crossing, they were both stunned by what they saw. A river of smooth, soundless water snaked through the valley. And set off from everything else, a cluster of hills stood, so tall they couldn't see the tops. In the center, the land inclined up toward the sky as though it was the ramp leading to something that hadn't arrived yet.

It was exactly what the man had hoped it'd be.

A path wound through the forest on one of the hills. They followed it, climbing higher and higher. At the top, the trees ended, and a grassy plateau began. It was the size of a city block, and since it was separated by deep canyons on all sides, it almost seemed to float several hundred feet above the valley floor. The effect was like being center stage in a giant theater in the middle of nowhere. He saw structures in the distance. It was here the people had built their town.

The settlement was much larger than the man had imagined.

It had thirty homes, each the size of a bungalow. There was even a small main street, built the old way: for foot traffic, not cars. Everything, though, led to the church at the end of town. Most churches had a prim, upright look that the man had never been able to stand. This church was different. It had been constructed with unpainted wood and was minimal and sophisticated yet old-seeming. It possessed no aspirations for greatness.

The man couldn't stop staring at it.

Only people who believed in something could have built such a place.

He and the boy explored the miniature homes. Some of the doors were locked. The boy wanted to kick one in, but the homes were neat, as if someone still loved them, and the man decided they should be left alone.

Most of the houses were bare, but something had been left behind in each of them. A doll, a shoe, books. What amazed the man was that the books were just like the ones he liked to read. There were the big important books that expand a person. Books on history. The meaning of life. All the things a person is desperate to know before it's too late.

There was also a book about writing a novel. Like most people, its owner felt he had a book in him. Probably he did. But like most people, he never wrote it. And so the book would die when he did.

Last but not least, there was a book about an old hunting club. The man fanned through pictures of an annual gala held every summer from 1920 to 1980. The man looked at everyone's smiling faces. They were almost all dead now.

The boy found toys that he'd played with himself. Pokémon cards. A remote control car.

They walked through the homes for hours. They were so absorbed that sometimes they'd get turned around and suddenly find themselves at the edge of town, only twenty feet from the canyons and their jagged cliffs.

The eeriness the man felt, the aloneness, was almost out-of-body. The surrounding hills towered over the town on three sides. But then to the north was the ramp he'd seen when they arrived. And at the end of the ramp was nothing, just wide-open sky. And when the man stared out, he saw the world of northern lights and polar vortexes. He saw the end of the known universe and the beginning of whatever came next.

One of the houses had mattresses on the beds, so they decided to move in. The man checked the water in the cistern. To his surprise, it was clear. When he turned on the tap, brown water sputtered out, but it soon ran clean.

"Here." He offered a cup to the boy. "Take a sip."

The boy tried it. "Tastes like socks."

The man tried some too. Then it was time.

They'd saved the church for last.

The man expected the doors to be locked. But they opened with ease. And somehow he wasn't surprised. It was as though the people here had built something so special to them that they just couldn't deny entry to anyone else.

The man and the boy walked the pews, leafing through the hymn books. The boy asked if it was okay to go up to the altar, and the man said yes. The man went over to the lectern. He found notes from the pastor's last sermon.

> I've stood before you for almost a decade, trying to be your spiritual guide. But I want you all to know the truth. After the tragedy that's happened and is still happening, I don't want to hear any words of consolation or wisdom. I want us to work together to get the hell out of here.

The man grinned, admiring the man behind these words. And then he remembered that the townspeople hadn't made it out of here. Everything good these people had been, it still hadn't been enough.

The boy's pain came back that night, stronger than before.

The man gave him another pill, but the boy kept asking in the humble, apologetic way of children for him to please do more. The man gave him a second dose and prayed it would work. Soon the boy became still, and the man realized he'd fallen asleep.

In the morning, it was the same thing. The boy woke up in agony, and the man was grateful they'd brought far more pills than they ever thought they needed.

CHAPTER

THE BOY'S PAIN soon required more than what was written on the bottles, and the man began giving him twice, then three times, the recommended dose. The boy's pain could have been kept at bay with less, but the man realized the more he overdosed his son, the more the boy could continue being himself.

By now, they'd explored the town. Still they never spoke of leaving.

Their favorite time was sunset. They'd walk around the town at golden hour, and they'd chat about this or that. One day, they heard clawing sounds on rock. Worried it might be another bear, they got their rifles and rushed outside.

It was a giant buck. They spotted it right as it walked behind the next ridge. The boy and the man followed. When the animal reappeared, it stood silhouetted only by orange sky.

"Do you want some meat?" the man asked.

Without answering, the boy took aim. The man waited, but

the boy never fired.

He took his eye off the scope as the buck disappeared from sight.

"Why didn't you shoot?" the man asked.

"He was magnificent. I just couldn't take that from him."

The boy didn't eat dinner that night. The next morning, he didn't want breakfast either.

It happened fast after that.

They stayed up talking the next two nights. It was almost impossible, the man realized, to talk normally with someone who'd only live a few more days. The future was just too hard not to speak of. And the man and the boy kept accidentally discussing things the boy would never again see.

Each night, after the boy had fallen asleep, the man would stay up and watch his son. He'd watch him and think.

They found a videotape in the church.

The man also discovered a VCR connected to a windup battery. After turning the crank for half an hour, he got the VCR to power on.

He and the boy exchanged amused looks.

He put in the tape. There was static, then shots of people preparing for a Christmas celebration.

"Hi," a woman said to the camera. "We're just getting our-selves ready for tonight."

"Really ready," another woman said, holding up a giant glass of wine.

Both of the women laughed.

They had laughs that made you like them right away.

The video cut to grainy footage taken inside the church, right where the man and the boy now stood. It was dark, and the church was filled with people holding candles. A chorus group of women and girls stood in the front. Some of them gig-gled nervously. Then the moment came. And they all changed somehow.

When they began to sing, the man and the boy both froze.

They performed "O Holy Night," but the man had never heard it sung that way before. There was one line they hit hard-er than the others and in fact sang with everything they had.

Fall on your knees.

And the way the women sang it, it was wistful and tragic, something rising from the deepest sorrow there was. And yet it was so beautiful it hurt. They sang those words as though they were the only possible reaction to such decency and grace. And the man understood the truth—that none of it was his. Not his life. Not his son. Not any of it. And he found that he too wanted to fall to his knees. He too wanted to be small, to be loved. And he wanted there to be good. As he stood next to his son, all he wanted was for there to be something good.

The boy woke up the next morning vomiting.

When he was finished, there were no jokes or gallows humor. And the man could tell he was fading.

"Listen," the man said, "I want to talk to you one last time before it's too late."

"Okay."

"You've been asking me about God and dying and what it all means. You've asked me how people can stand to live when we know so little. And I just want to tell you something."

The boy looked at him, totally blank, totally open.

The man grabbed him and spoke through gritted teeth. "I don't know if there's a god. I don't know if there's a heaven. I don't know if anything we do counts for a goddamn thing. Maybe we're just another species waiting to go extinct. But what I do know is this: I *want* there to be a god. I *want* for all this to have meant something. And more than anything, I want for something out there to see all the goodness in here." He touched the boy's chest. "To see what I see."

"What if it doesn't?"

"Then all I know is that I love you. And if you don't matter to whatever's out there, then fuck whatever's out there. Because you matter to me. You understand?" He'd grabbed the boy's shoulder and was shaking it. "You're all that matters to me. You're the only thing left I still believe in."

The man paused, exhaling, as he regained his senses.

"You're the son I always wanted," he said. "I never told you this. But I used to picture what it'd be like to have a son. And it's even better than I hoped."

"Really? Even though I died?"

"Yes."

The boy was watching him intently.

"You want to know something else?" the man said. "I'll never let you go. Maybe this place is going to kill you, but I won't let it kill you completely. No matter what, you'll always live in me."

They hugged, grasping each other as if they'd never let go, as if something was attempting to separate them.

The man thought they'd stay like that forever. But soon his arms got tired and the boy's did too. So they did what ten minutes earlier had been unthinkable, and they let go of each other.

The man never left the boy after that. His biggest fear was that the boy would die while he was out gathering wood. It was almost unthinkable, the thought of the child dying alone.

There was also something else.

The man wanted to be close by because he didn't know if death really was the end. And if some part of him could pass over with the boy, he wanted to be there for whatever was coming for his son.

"Dad, it's happening."

The man rushed over.

The boy's face was stricken. "I'm not ready."

"Listen to me. They say that people fight it when they're with a loved one. But I don't want you to fight it anymore."

"I don't want to go anywhere. I want to stay here with you."

"I know."

"I'm so scared."

"I'm not scared," the man said, lying. "Because we're going to do it together."

"I really wanted to go back to that little diner." The boy took a labored breath. "I want to see Mom and Sid."

The man said nothing.

"It's all gone now, isn't it?"

"That's right. Now it's just you and me."

The boy nodded, accepting what he had to.

For a time, they just laid there together, existing.

"It's happening again," the boy said.

"What?"

But the boy didn't reply.

And no matter how tight the man held him, he began to slip away.

"I'm still here," the man said. "I'm not going anywhere."

The boy nodded, but some part of him had already passed over. His eyes stared at something, just not something the man could see. The man never left his side. He hugged him and kept talking to him even as the boy's face began to slacken.

When the boy was dead, the man continued speaking to him. He thought of the movie the boy told him about, the one where a man died and woke up in the woods. The man wondered if his son was in those woods, powerless against whatever would be done to him. He wondered if the boy could hear his father's voice in the distance and knew his father could no longer help him.

The man buried the boy in the yard next to the church.

When he lowered the boy down, the boy's arms bunched up so he was hugging himself. His face had a look of such rest that the man couldn't stop staring at it. He wasn't a body yet. He was a boy accidentally trapped behind the paper-thin barrier separating life and death.

The man stepped out of the grave and sat for a few hours. Then he began to push dirt in.

He covered the boy's face last. Dirt pooled around the boy's eye sockets. Then everything was covered except his nostrils.

When the man was finished, he went behind the church. The land there jutted out like a pulpit, and the surrounding hills towered over him. He stood alone and humbled and wide-open. And the immensity of it all hit him until he thought his chest would burst. He looked at the church and prayed that what those people believed was true. He prayed that his son was more than a student filling a seat. He prayed that he wasn't just a little boy with crushed hopes and broken dreams who'd already been everything he was ever going to be.

He went a little mad then, arguing and pleading with things that weren't there. He had thoughts powerful enough to kill a person. After a while, it all vanished, and he could see what was right in front of him. He was just a man sitting by himself in the middle of nowhere.

When the man woke the next morning, he looked at his hands and body, surprised somehow that he was still alive.

His eyes stopped on his rifle. If there was an afterlife and it was terrible, the boy had no one to protect him. The man thought about that a long time.

He went out and gathered wood. He had no intention of leaving, but the town no longer interested him now that the boy was gone. That evening, the man made one last fire and sat by himself. His sorrow ran so deep he began to feel gratitude—that he'd ever gotten time with the boy at all. He spent the night there and also the next night. He left only because he ran out of food.

Before leaving, he fashioned a crude headstone out of some sticks. It wasn't right. So he drove the boy's rifle deep into the ground with a rock. Then he tied his own rifle across it, forming a cross.

As he hiked out of the valley, he kept turning and looking back. He made it another ten miles before he realized the danger of what he'd done. He was out of supplies, and he'd left his gun behind. By the time he made it to Hanover, he was on the verge of exhaustion.

The town looked the exact same as before. He bought food at the convenience store and got a room. He ate and then collapsed on the bed. It was early evening when he woke. He showered and shaved, and when he looked in the mirror, it was as though none of it had ever happened. All except for his eyes. He had the eyes of someone who'd seen things a person was never meant to understand.

He walked over to the diner. All the regulars were still there.

But when they looked at his face and saw the boy wasn't with him, no one spoke. The entire place fell silent. The man ordered food and sat eating. He'd had every intention of buying more supplies, another gun, and going back up into the high country. But then he froze—because he realized in horror that he couldn't.

What he and the boy had come here for was no longer here.

He sat dabbing French fries with ketchup. He stared out the window at the hills. Already the country looked different.

The people around him were discussing the weather and their evening plans. He didn't know how he kept his composure and didn't start smashing things. But he continued to eat. After a time, the man thought of his wife and daughter back at home, two souls waiting for him to return.

"Excuse me," he said to the waitress. "Is there a taxi here or something?"

"Sure. Where are you going?"

"An airport."

As the taxi left, the man looked at Montana one last time. He thought of the boy and what they'd done together. The boy no longer existed, yet he was still out there somewhere. In some way, he couldn't be erased. And the man thought, *Life has defeated us all. But it hasn't defeated us entirely.*